TANGLED UP IN YOU

Evergreen Valley Holidays
Book 1.5

SHANNON O'CONNOR

Cover by *Graphics by Stacy*.

Edited by *Cruel Ink Editing & Design*.

Proofread by Victoria Ellis of *Cruel Ink Editing & Design*.

Formatted by Shannon O'Connor.

❀ Formatted with Vellum

Hands On Me - Jason Derulo ft. Meghan Trainor

A Nonsense Christmas - Sabrina Carpenter

santa doesn't know you like I do - Sabrina Carpenter

Stupid for You - Waterparks

Very Merry - Anna Mae

Wrap Me Up - Bellah Mae

Snow Angel - Elli Moore

she got a thing about her - Thomas Day

Like it's Christmas - Jonas Brothers

For all the single moms who are waiting for a Parker to come into their lives & find out where they fit.

ONE

Tessa

———

"**D**o you remember what I told both of you?" I ask.

"Don't yell, try to keep busy, and keep an eye on Drew," my oldest daughter Natalie says.

At the same time, Drew, my youngest, shouts, "Don't pick my nose! And stay with Nat!" He smiles proudly, but then his finger returns to his nose. When he sees me looking at him through the rearview mirror, he immediately takes it out and rubs it on his shirt. *Lovely.*

"It's only for the next two weeks, then you'll be back in school. I promise I'll have time off or a babysitter when you have your next break from school," I remind Natalie. She's only thirteen, and while I trust her to stay home alone, I worry too much about leaving both of them. So for now, they have to come to work with me at the Evergreen Valley Public Library, and Natalie watches Drew there.

"I know, Mom. It's fine. I'm already ordering the new clothes you said I could buy if I do a good job." She smiles as she looks up from her cell phone. I reluctantly gave in when she asked for a phone. It's a good way to keep in touch with her when she's at her dad's, and it's also nice for her to be able to talk directly to him using her phone. I'd rather not communicate with him more than I have to. I'll stick to speaking with him through our lawyers.

"You're buying them already?" I raise an eyebrow.

"Well yeah, if I wait, they might not come in time for my first day of school." She flashes her braces at me, and I sigh.

"Okay, fine. Now, let's go," I say, motioning for her to get out of the car.

Grabbing my travel cup filled with tea, my work bag, and lunch bag, I step out of the car. I place the lunch box on the roof of my car, unbuckle Drew from his seat, and he hops out next to me into the snow. It's the gross kind of snow that's all black and dirty from days of being walked through. We've only been in town a few days and have yet to experience the pretty white snow. Drew puts his coat back on—even though it's only a short walk inside—and I help him with his backpack. It's full of things for him and Natalie to do today so he isn't tempted to spend the day playing Minecraft on his tablet.

Drew takes my hand, and we all walk into the oversized brick building. It looks old, like it's been here since the town was originally founded. The front door is up a set of steps that look just as old. But inside everything is sleek and modern. The walls are pale, there are new computers in a row, and everything looks extra clean. The director mentioned there was a recent update, but since our interview was on Zoom, this is the first I'm seeing it in person.

"Hello! Welcome! I'm Paige. How can I help you?" a woman sitting at the circulation desk asks. She has short, curly, dark hair with long eyelashes and plump pink lips. She can't be more than twenty-one or twenty-two.

"Hi, it's actually my first day. I'm Tessa Williams." I smile, extending my free hand to her.

"Oh! Yes, Dawn said you'd be coming in today. She's in her office just down that way, are these your kids?" Paige smiles.

"Yes. Natalie and Drew. Dawn said they can hang around here until they start school. I just moved to town, so I don't have a babysitter yet," I explain.

"No problem! Do you guys want me to show you the rec room? There isn't anyone in there today, so you can hang in there, and you don't have to worry about the noise," Paige suggests.

I nod. "That would be awesome. Thank you so much."

"Don't stress! I'll show them where it is, and you can go see Dawn," Paige says. I look at Natalie, who nods encouragingly.

"Okay, thank you." I smile and head in the direction she pointed.

Through stacks of library books and shelves, I find an office at the end of the hallway. Dawn's name is engraved on the nameplate next to the door, along with the words *library director*. The door is cracked open, so I lightly tap on the wood and wait for her to answer.

"Tessa! Oh, it's so great to meet in person!" She smiles cheerfully. She has bright red curls that seem to fall in every which way. "I hope you found the town okay. It's your first time here right?"

"Yes, we just got to town a few days ago. But so far, everyone has been very kind and welcoming." Natalie said the town reminds her of a place where a Hallmark movie would be filmed. I'm still not entirely sure if she meant that as an insult or not.

"That's lovely! Okay, so follow me, and I'll show you to your office." Dawn grabs her keys—a pink carabiner shaped like a heart with a multitude of keys on the ring.

Dawn leads me around the corner to an office that looks the same as hers from the outside, but on the nameplate next to the door it says my name. *Tessa Williams, Library Program Director.* It's one of the first times I've seen my maiden name used recently. I decided to go back to using it again, now that the divorce is finalized; it just feels right. It's just weird not sharing a last name with my kids anymore. I still haven't legally changed it yet, but when Dawn asked, I knew I wanted my maiden name on the door—not my ex's name. He doesn't deserve any part of my new life.

"Here you go! This is your key, and there's a set to open and close the library. Please do not copy or lose the key. If you do, there will be a fee, and it's a lot of extra paperwork," Dawn says, handing me a small keyring. "Your hours are firm, as we discussed, but I'm flexible with you bringing your kids with you. My mom was a single mother, and I know working was a challenge without having close family. I'd rather you come in and have them with you then not come in at all."

"Thank you. That will help a ton. They'll be starting school after winter break, and I just don't feel comfortable with them at home by themselves, especially in a new area they aren't familiar with," I say.

"Don't worry about it." Dawn smiles and unlocks my office door, and I look around in complete awe.

The walls are grey, but there's a white L-shaped desk that takes up half the room. The other side is filled with empty bookshelves and miscellaneous office supplies. I can definitely see the potential. All I need to do is bring in the artwork from my old office, photos of my kids, and a few other miscellaneous items— then it'll be perfect.

"There's a stack of paper with events awaiting approval for the new year. Our last program director left in a bit of hurry, so I apologize if they're in disarray." Dawn sighs, her brows dipping.

"No problem at all. I'm sure I can figure it out." I smile, setting down my stuff on the desk.

"I'll leave you to get settled. There's a staff meeting today at noon, and you'll meet everyone there. Otherwise, if you have any questions, please just let me know." Dawn smiles and I nod.

As soon as she leaves, I take out my phone and track Natalie. I know she's still in the building, but I want to make sure the map is still working. I have a bit of anxiety when it comes to my kids—especially lately. I'm sure it's because of the divorce, but my therapist assured me it's totally normal. I like knowing I can find them in an emergency if need be. Once I know she's a safe distance away, I put my phone back in my bag and start unpacking.

I'll need to bring more from home, but I haven't even unpacked all of our boxes yet. I focused on Natalie and Drew's room, and then the kitchen and living room. My room is still filled with the most unopened boxes, because I know how to live without much. I take out my work keyboard, laptop, pencil case, and headphones. I place my favorite photo of Natalie holding Drew as a baby on the corner of my desk and take a sip of my coffee. I go through the office supplies, weeding out items that look overly used or things I simply don't need. I'll donate a lot of it. I enjoy keeping my space clear, and I can't do that with a million things I'd never use.

"Hey! Your kids are adorable, by the way," Paige says poking her head in. I gasp, clutching my chest in surprise. "Sorry, I should really announce myself. I know I can be a little hyper."

"It's okay. I was just deep in thought," I lie. She should definitely come with a bell or something.

"I dropped them off in the rec room, and Natalie said to tell you they're fine. Drew was running around with a makeshift sword, and Natalie was timing him," Paige explains.

"Got it." I nod. They're probably playing some made up game. Drew is creative and usually keeps us on our toes. We're always learning how to play new games he's thought up.

"Did Dawn give you a tour of the place? Or just show you your office?" Paige asks.

"Oh, actually just my office." I frown.

"Come on, I give a pretty great tour." Paige says with a big smile.

I follow her through the library where she points out the different sections. Then she shows me the break room, which has a full-size fridge and sink, along with a small table and a set of lockers. She brings me to the circulation desk, where someone else is helping a patron check out. She explains the checkout process—which is the same system my old job used. It'll be rare for me to check anyone out, but it's good to know just in case. Paige brings me to the kids section of the library and then finally to the rec room, which is a bit detached from the main space.

"Mama!" Drew's voice carries from the other side of the room where he's holding a paper sword and his favorite stuffed penguin.

"Hi baby, how's it going?" I smile as he crashes against my legs.

"Is it time to go home?" He looks up at me with hopeful eyes, and my heart breaks just a little. I wish I could take him home now and spend the day playing with him. It's been awhile since I've worked. I've been home with the kids for quite a long time, so this will take some getting used to.

"Not yet." I frown, ruffling the hair on his head.

"I thought we were still playing, Drew?" Natalie calls from where she's sitting on the floor with some blocks.

"Oh yeah! Bye, Mama!" Drew runs back over to his big sister, setting down his sword to finish building with the blocks. Natalie smiles at me, silently reassuring me that all is fine. I know she understands my hesitation. When Natalie started school, I went back to work. But once I had Drew, I stayed home again. I loved every second of it.

It's hard—getting into the swing of things while recognizing how different things are going to be. Now that I'm divorced, things are different…not only for me, but for the kids too. I anticipated the big changes, like moving and starting to work again. But it's the little changes that sometimes hit me harder. Things like knowing I can't be a frequent PTA volunteer this year and knowing I won't have the extra time to make things for their bake sales or attend all of the school functions. Our house might be full of boxes for the next few months, honestly. I'm going to be super busy. Unpacking is pretty low on my to-do list right now.

I just hope I know what I'm doing...

I feel like I'm caught up in a mess of my own making—like tangled Christmas lights.

TWO

Parker

By the time I crawl out of bed, I know it must be pretty late in the day. I was up until six in the morning, working out the coding of a new app, and I didn't want to sleep until it was done. It's not the first time my job's kept me up so late, and I honestly don't mind it. It isn't like I usually have anything to do or somewhere to go during the day. But as I groggily wipe the crust off my eyes and let out a long yawn, I know it's later than normal. I grab my phone from the charger and realize it's 4:30 p.m.

Stretching, I headed downstairs to the kitchen and flip on the coffee pot. My kitchen is a bit of a mess, with dishes overflowing and two-day-old food sitting on them. I've been on deadline, and everything else has fallen through the cracks. But now it's off my plate, and besides a little maintenance here or there, I'm done with projects until the new year.

I turn on the sink, letting the water get hot, and then I clean all the dishes. I have a dishwasher, but honestly, I don't know how to use it. I normally just keep snacks in there. Once all the dishes are clean and dry, I wipe off the counters and make myself a fresh cup of coffee. I pour in three scoops of sugar and a splash of milk before I hear someone banging outside. Peering out the front window, I can't see much, so I slip on my fuzzy slippers and open the door to my front porch. It snowed again, but I'll be fine on the porch; it's covered, and I don't mind the cold.

I turn my head to the side and see a woman standing on a ladder. She's putting up Christmas lights. I recognize her as my new neighbor, although I haven't officially met her yet. I heard them moving in earlier this week, and it wasn't a surprise. The old lady who lived there moved to Florida to buy a vacation home with her longtime girlfriend. I clearly don't know much about these neighbors yet, but she's apparently pretty into Christmas. As she steps down from the ladder, my heart skips a beat.

Long dark hair flows freely behind her—all the way down her back in perfect loose curls. Her cheekbones are tight, pink because of the cold, and laugh lines sit near her eyes and the corners of her mouth. She is definitely older than I am, but she doesn't look old. She is wearing a dark red coat that hangs from her thin frame, and a pair of black leggings that show off the perfectly round ass she is not attempting to hide. Her dark eyes catch mine only for a second before looking back at the work she has done. Holy hell. How can this woman be this freaking beautiful?

"Hi!" She waves and shouts loudly.

I'm suddenly very aware of the fact that I'm in my pajamas. And not a cute matching set, but an old T-shirt that says 'I've got connections' with drawings of USB connectors and a pair of sweatpants older than I am. They have paint stains and holes all over the place. This is *not* how I wanted to meet her.

"Hi!" I smile, hoping maybe she won't come over.

But then I see her hopping off her front porch and walking down the path that connects our houses. I brace myself—maybe she isn't *that* hot. Then she steps onto my porch, and I lose my breath. How is she even hotter up close? Doesn't that defy the laws of physics or something?

"I'm Tessa! We just moved in next door—my kids and I." She holds out her hand, and I almost spill my coffee attempting to reach for her.

"Hi, I'm Polly Parker. But everyone calls me Parker—well, except when I was called *PP* in elementary school."

I watch as she bites her bottom lip, clearly trying not to laugh. What the hell is wrong with me?! Why would I tell her that? Better question is, were my parents drunk when they came up with my name? My initials are literally PP. Just imagine telling that to a group of kids. Growing up with those initials was literal torture. Every time someone wanted to talk about nicknames or initials, it came up.

Now, I usually just introduce myself as Parker, but something about her is making me nervous.

"Mom!" a teenager in front of Tessa's house calls. I'm assuming that's her daughter.

"What?" she shouts back.

"Drew wants a snack! Can he have Cheetos?" the teen shouts again.

"Yes!" Tessa yells then turns back to me. "Sorry about that. That's my daughter Natalie, and I have a four-year-old, Drew."

"Nice." I gesture to my house. "It's just me here," I say shyly.

"We also have a new dog, but she's trained, so hopefully she won't bother you," Tessa reassures me.

"I love dogs!" I blurt out. It's like all my flirting skills just evaporated. Maybe it's due to my lack of sleep, but I have a feeling my sudden lack of brain cells has more to do with the gorgeous woman standing in front of me.

"Mom! Drew wants you!" her daughter calls again.

"Sorry, mom duties call. It was nice meeting you, Parker!" Tess smiles, and I melt a little.

Thankfully, I compose myself enough to get back inside before I melt completely. How the hell is she so beautiful? She radiates confidence and sexiness I've only seen older women have. It's like they're just so at peace with who they are that they don't give a fuck about anything else. Of course I know better than to shit where I eat. I'm not going to make a move on my neighbor, that would just be crazy, right? It would make things awkward at the next block party, that's for sure. And I like our block parties.

I take a sip of my now-cold coffee, then head back to the kitchen and pop it back into the microwave. I glance out the window near my living room and see Tessa has returned to putting up her lights. God, she must do Pilates or squats every day to have an ass like that. I wonder if she's going to the gym in town now. I haven't seen her there, but it's been a bit since I've gone. The app has taken over my life lately—except for helping Jax with the bookstore fundraiser. Her family's bookstore is in danger of eviction because of a decades-old feud. She came up with the idea to do an event to raise the money to keep it open. I've been doing everything possible to help her, but I'm nervous it won't be enough.

I grab my hot cup of coffee and head back upstairs to my room. My phone buzzes on my dresser, and I realize someone's calling me.

"Hello?"

"Are you coming over? I thought you'd be here already," Shiloh, my other best friend, says.

"Oh crap, did we have plans?" I groan.

"I thought we were doing our yearly tradition of watching all the holiday episodes of *Bob's Burgers*?" Shiloh asks.

"Uh yes. Give me thirty minutes. I need to shower and find my Christmas pajamas." I look around the room, hoping they'll magically appear. Shiloh and I got matching ones at the beginning of the season, but I can't recall where I put them. I'm usually more put together and organized, but right now, everything is a mess.

"We can reschedule if you need…"

"No! I'm coming, but trust me, this shower is as much for you as it is for me." I laugh.

"Okay, text me when you're on your way," Shiloh says before hanging up.

I look for the pjs first, figuring I don't want to be naked and cold looking for them after my shower. After tidying up my room a bit, I find them in my closet still in the bag we bought them in. I pull off the labels and head for the shower. I scrub myself clean and only come out when I smell as good as I look. I toss on the pajamas and head for the car.

I know Shiloh probably won't care how I look or smell, but *I* care. Shiloh is one of my oldest friends—besides Jax. Shiloh and I dated in college during freshman year, and when we broke up we stayed friends…the way lesbians seem to do. We hooked up randomly for a while, but we ultimately decided it was better for us to just be friends. She's probably seen and smelled me at my worst, honestly, but I like to be as put together as possible.

Shiloh lives a few blocks away with her roommate, Jade. The front door is open when I get there, so I let myself in, kick off my snowy boots, and look around for Shiloh.

"It's about time! I was getting bored," she says, tossing her phone on the couch and jumping up to hug me.

"I'm sorry. I was up late working. But now I'm off until the new year." I smile.

"That's amazing!"

"Is Jax coming?" I didn't have a chance to check the group chat to see.

"No, apparently she's still in the city." Shiloh shrugs.

"I think she's with El."

"WHAT?!" Shiloh screams. "Tell me everything!"

"I don't know much. I just know I caught them making out in the closet when we worked on fundraiser stuff. And I saw Jax's boob, which was not high on my list of sights to see." I groan. Jax and I are like siblings, I don't want to think of her boobs.

"Holy shit. This is insane. Forbidden lovers!" Shiloh says, romanticizing things as usual.

"I guess." I shrug.

"How do you know they're together this weekend?"

"El lives in the city. Jax mentioned going there to see how El lives to make sure it's suitable for their cat," I explain.

"They got a cat together!? Well if that isn't textbook lesbians." Shiloh laughs.

"Well, El found the cat outside the bookstore, and they've been taking care of it. But they couldn't agree on where the cat should live. So supposedly Jax is there to see El's apartment, but I don't buy it."

"Oh no way. They're totally fucking." Shiloh nods.

"I think they're good together, but I know Jax is hesitant because of who her family is." I sigh.

"It's not like she can't handle herself. It's nice to see Jax actually getting some for once though," Shiloh says.

I nod in agreement. Shiloh stops in the kitchen to grab some chips and wine and a Diet Coke for me since I have to drive home eventually. We watch the episodes in order; I like the newer ones better, but Shiloh likes the older ones. Even though we do this every year, we laugh at all the funny parts like it's our first time seeing it.

In the back of my mind, I'm wondering if Tessa likes *Bob's Burgers* and what she's up to tonight. I've never been this curious about someone I just met—let alone with someone who has children. It isn't a good idea to get involved with her. But she's definitely going to live in my fantasies, that's for sure. Her perfectly round ass is all I can think about. I wonder what she looks like without that winter coat on. I bet she has the best body. It's only been a few weeks since I hooked up with someone, but I'm so fucking horny for Tess.

Parker's shoveling the snow again. I didn't know it could snow so many times in one week. I never really paid attention to it until I was the one responsible for it. I've been out there three times this week, and it feels like I can't keep up. The kids helped clean off the car since we don't have a garage. But I'm stuck making a path for us to walk and drive out of. Not exactly what I want to be doing when I'm coming home from work exhausted.

"Did you get any rock salt?" Parker asks. She's all bundled up. I can barely see anything except her face through the hood, but she's still hot.

"Rock salt?" I must look puzzled, because Parker laughs. Not in a way that's making fun of me, but in an *aw cute* sort of way.

"I have some extra if you need. I noticed you having a hard time with the ice earlier. That can happen if the snow melts and freezes, but if you put down rock salt it's less likely," she explains.

"Oh, yeah I don't have any of that." I frown. Another thing to add to the shopping list.

"Mine is pet safe, not all of them are though. So just be

careful of that when you buy them. I wouldn't want your dog to eat it and get sick," Parker says.

"Thank you, that's really good to know."

Parker walks to her porch, grabs a cup, and comes back to the path I'd been digging out. "You only need a sprinkled layer. You can put more, but then it gets stuck in your shoes." She sprinkles it over the path, and I look at it curiously.

"I know it doesn't look like much, but I swear it helps." She laughs.

"I haven't even unpacked everything yet, let alone picked up everything I need for the house."

"No worries, if you need it and I'm not here, I keep it on the porch right there. Feel free to help yourself." She smiles.

"Thank you, Parker. I really appreciate it. I thought moving to a small town would be like the movies. I figured I'd run into someone I could pay to shovel for me. But at least I'm getting to know my neighbor," I say.

"Where did you move from?" Parker asks as she continues putting down the rock salt.

"Boston. It's been a bit of a culture shock for us. We're getting used to the small town ways of things," I explain.

"Did you move for a job?" Parker pauses. "Sorry if that's too personal. Feel free to tell me to go home."

"No, it's okay. I moved for a job—and because I recently got divorced. Their father and I separated, and I thought a new town and job would be a nice fresh start," I explain.

"That's awesome! I hope they like it. I was born and raised here. Probably going to die here one day, too," Parker says with a big smile.

"You love this town that much?" I try not to sound judgmental, but I don't think I do a great job disguising my voice.

"I do. I know it may not seem like much, but the people in this town all come together when you need them. We're a small community with a lot of heart," she says proudly.

"I see." I don't yet, but I hope I will eventually because that's exactly what I was looking for when we decided to move here.

"By the way, do you go to the gym around here?" Parker asks.

"No, not yet, anyway. Why?"

"I was just curious what your workout routine is. I hope this isn't creepy, but you're gorgeous." Parker winks. My cheeks flush, or they would if they weren't already bright pink from the cold.

"Now why would I mind that? I used to do Zumba a few times a week, but lately it's just all this snow shoveling." I laugh.

"Well then, I guess I'm not shoveling the right way, because I know I've never looked like you." She bites down on her bottom lip and looks me over in a way that sends a shiver down my spine. Is she flirting with me?

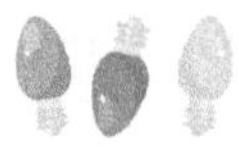

"Did you know that there are sheep in Minecraft?" Drew asks from his car seat.

"I didn't know that. I thought the movie had chickens."

"It does! Lava chicken!" Drew starts singing that God awful song from the movie. I don't know how this movie is so popular. It plays at least once a day in our house."

Natalie is tuned out in the front seat with her headphones on. I'm giving her grace with them, even though the car is usually a family space for us to talk. But lately she's been helping out so much with Drew while I'm at work, so I want to give back a little. In two short weeks, she'll be back in school and the responsibilities will change, but I want to give her time to have fun being a kid too. She isn't going to become my permanent built-in babysitter just because she's the older sister. That's how she'll end up resenting me and not talking to me as an adult. I know better. I'm already on the hunt for a certified babysitter or nanny in the area who can take care of Drew.

"Alright, go wash up for dinner," I say as I pull into the driveway. Natalie unbuckles Drew and takes my key to unlock the front door.

As I get out of my car, I realize someone's shoveled the driveway. Gone is the fresh snow I was cursing when I saw it outside my office window. Instead, there's a fresh sprinkle of the rock salt stuff, and I can actually see the driveway pavement. It's like someone answered my prayers...

"Hey." A woman's voice startles me as I'm grabbing our groceries out of the trunk.

"Oh, hey." I smile at my beautiful neighbor.

"Do you need any help?" Parker asks as she sees me struggling to grab all the bags and close the trunk.

"Yes, thank you," I say, but she already has three bags on her arms and is closing the trunk for me. Damn, she's fast.

"I can bring them in, if that's okay with you. Unless you'd rather I leave them out here?" she asks hesitantly. I appreciate the choice.

"You can come in. It's probably a mess, but please come in." I laugh. She probably isn't a serial killer.

Hopefully.

She follows me through the living room to the back of the house where the kitchen is. She places the bags down on the kitchen table and looks at me.

"Thanks, I'm sorry. I'd invite you to stay, but the place is a mess, and I have to cook, and—"

"Don't worry about it. I was actually hoping to take you to dinner." Parker smiles, and like a movie star, she has a twinkle in her eye.

Her hair is down today, showcasing her long red locks. She's only wearing a bit of makeup, but it makes her blue eyes pop. As she stands next to me, I realize she's shorter than I initially thought—almost a good five inches shorter than me. There's no denying her beauty. Even when I saw her in ratty old pajamas and with bedhead that looked like it hadn't been brushed in days, she was gorgeous.

"Dinner?" I ask, realizing I need to respond.

"Yes or lunch. Whichever you prefer." She chuckles nervously.

"Like a date?" I try not to wince. Maybe I'm reading things wrong.

"Yes." She nods.

"No."

"No?" She looks at me, clearly surprised.

"No. I'm sorry." I sigh. "I have two kids and a full-time job; I barely have enough time to eat, let alone go on a date right now. But I appreciate you asking." I smile.

"Are you only saying no because of that? Or because you're not attracted to me?" Parker asks, tilting her head.

"I'm attracted to you." I keep my voice low, but I feel like my words come out a bit unsteady.

"Good, then this won't be the last time I ask you."

"I'm going to have to say no every time. I just don't have the time or energy to date right now." I sigh.

"Okay, we'll see how things go." Parker shrugs and heads out the front door.

I stare after her, puzzled. Part of me wants to go over to her house and yell at her. How dare she tell me *we'll see how things go*. I know what I do and do not have time for. I barely have time to pee and sleep, how could I have a new relationship right now? But the other part of me knows she doesn't mean it the way a man would. She's not trying to change my mind; it seems like, if anything, she's hoping *I'll* change my mind. I don't know if I mind seeing how she plans on making that happen.

"Mama are we having dinner?" Drew asks, snapping me from my spiral.

"Yes, I'm making dino nuggets and mac and cheese. Sound good?"

"Yes! Can I make a mountain of mac and cheese for the dinos to climb?" he asks, smiling.

"Of course!" I ruffle his hair, and he runs back into the living room where he's playing with his Legos.

Natalie isn't in sight, which means she's probably in her bedroom texting or FaceTiming her friends. I feel bad that I took her away from her friends in Boston, but she's social. An extrovert that can make friends anywhere. And I wanted to move her now, before she starts high school in the fall. Part of me wished they could've finished out the school year, but I couldn't hold off Weston selling the house any longer. He wanted the money from the sale to move on and buy a new house with his new wife. I'm not even salty about it, we'd had good times, but we both knew our marriage was over. The day he asked me for a divorce, I wasn't even surprised. He gave me the papers, and I signed without even consulting a lawyer. It was a simple negotiation: I wanted the kids and child support. He could have the house. For the last few years, we've barely spoken to each other, just walking through life as a necessity. Weston moved on, got remarried, and lives on the border of Connecticut now. He's close enough to eventually see the kids on the weekends...like we agreed.

It's hard when so much of my life was spent with him and the kids. It's like I'm rediscovering who I am by myself. He isn't a bad husband, but he also isn't the best. I never feel like we got married for the right reasons, eloping right after Natalie was born. And I never feel like I'm his wife, but more his mother or caretaker—constantly reminding him to do the dishes or change his underwear. A lot of taking care of the kids falls onto me, unless it's something fun. It's the unspoken reality that he's the fun parent and I'm the 'bad guy.' When in reality I'm the one making sure they have helmets on their bikes and lunches packed for school and clean underpants every day. I sure do not miss making sure a mediocre man is taking care of himself. And I sure as shit do not wish for him back. If anything, I pity his new wife—just knowing exactly what she's going through.

FOUR

Parker

"How are you so convinced you're going to get this woman to go out with you? You barely know her," Shiloh says, looking up from where she's painting my toenails a Christmas red.

"Because she just thinks she doesn't have time or doesn't think she should have a life. But all moms should. Trust me, I was raised by one." I shrug.

To me, it's obvious Tessa thinks she should be putting her kids first. And there is absolutely no shame in that. In every situation in the universe, the kids should come first. But I'm also a firm believer that single moms should be entitled to have a life outside of being a mom. My mother went out with her friends every Friday night, and I stayed with my grandparents. Sure, I missed her for a night, but every time she came to pick me up on Saturday afternoon, she had the biggest smile on her face. She seemed more relaxed than ever.

I'm definitely not trying to be a creeper, but I don't think I ever see Tessa going out with friends—or even having the kids leaving for a night. She's beautiful and sweet, and I want to get to know her better…in whatever capacity she let me.

"I agree with you," Jax says, looking up from the book she's reading. She isn't big on painting her nails or having a spa night, but she agreed to let us put a face mask on her while she's reading. I suppose that's a win.

"You do?" I ask, surprised.

"Yeah, I mean, if she said no because she wasn't attracted to you, then I'd say to back off. But if she wants to but is saying no because she thinks she doesn't have the time, maybe just show her how you can fit into the time she has available," Jax suggests.

"What do you mean?" Shiloh asks, beating me to the punch.

"You know that episode of *How I Met Your Mother* where Ted asks out Stella a bunch of times and she says no every single time?" We nod in unison. "But then he asks her on a two-minute date, because she says that's all the time she has for lunch. He doesn't give up and instead fits into her schedule and gives her a memorable time."

"Why are you only working at a bookstore and not writing romance novels?" Shiloh teases Jax.

"I enjoy the escape. But I'm serious. Doing things in her schedule shows her that you understand the time she has is valuable, and you don't want to waste it. Plus, it shows her you're serious. Considering the age gap, that might be helpful too," Jax adds.

"She's not *that* much older than me," I say.

"I've seen her, and she's at least ten years older," Shiloh says.

"So what? I'm mature for my age." I laugh.

"The only mature thing about you is the type of wine you drink," Jax jokes.

"Rude," I grumble.

Shiloh moves on to my fingernails, and I keep a close eye on how she does it. I don't want it to get messed up. I keep my nails longer, but not too long, because they get in the way of coding. Once my nails and toes match, I lean back on the couch and think about Tessa—and about what Jax said.

She's right. I should try to figure out how I can fit into her schedule or what I can do to help her. I shoveled the driveway for her yesterday while she was at work. She didn't say anything, but I know she noticed. When she said no, she mentioned how she never has time to eat. I could bring her over a quick meal. Maybe that'll help. I'm pretty good at making simple things. I can make lasagna, chicken cutlets, homemade mac and cheese, and most pasta variations. I don't know if Tessa or her kids have any allergies, but it's the thought that counts, right? I jump up and head to the kitchen to see what I have.

"Where are you going?" Shiloh calls from the couch.

"I wanna make dinner for Tessa. She's always exhausted after work, and she still has to make dinner for the kids. I think this is a way I could help out," I explain. I have noodles, tomato sauce, and frozen ground beef. I can make a mean lasagna. I dig through my cheese drawer and pull out the best kind for my recipe.

"Do you need help?" Jax asks, joining me in the kitchen with Shiloh.

"No, I'm okay, but thank you." I smile.

I wash my hands and start putting everything together. Shiloh, Jax, and I catch up about life. Shiloh went out with someone from a dating app last week who turned out to be her ex posing as someone else. They begged to get back together with her, and when Shiloh said no, they threw an iced coffee at her. I wish I could say that wasn't on brand for the crazy things that happen to her, but it totally is. She has a slew of crazy exes. Jax, on the other hand, is making moves with El. She won't say too much, but she has a small hickey on the side of her neck that proves all we need to know. It's so cute seeing my best friend get shy for the first time.

I glance at the clock and think about the lasagna. It's almost time for her to get home. I'm not a stalker, but she does seem to come home at the same time every day. I can cook it here and bring it over hot. She won't have to do anything but serve it. I set the timer on the clock and rip the ingredient list labels off of all the things I used. I set everything in a pile and make a mental note to bring them with me when I head over. I'm aware of allergies, and I want to make sure Tess knows everything in the lasagna just in case.

"I have to get home. Grandma's making dinner," Jax says, packing up her book.

"Me too," Shiloh says.

"You too?" I raise an eyebrow.

"Well, my grandma isn't cooking. But I am going over to Jax's to steal food. I've been living off Door Dash, and it's sad when it's the same person every night delivering my food." Shiloh sighs. It's one of the downfalls of living in a small town. For the longest time, we didn't even have Door Dash as an option.

"Have fun!" I laugh while they head out.

While I'm waiting for the lasagna to finish cooking, I head upstairs to change. I want to look cute, but not like I'm trying too hard. I decide to put on a pair of leggings and a cute sweater, letting my hair down, even though I'll throw on a hat before going over. My makeup is already done, so now I just need to wait for them to get home.

Twenty minutes later, the timer has three minutes left on the clock, and I hear a car pulling up Tessa's driveway. Peeking into the oven, I realize the lasagna looks perfect, so I grab it with oven mitts and place it on the counter. I quickly put my shoes, jacket, and hat on before grabbing the lasagna and making my way over.

I knock on the door and hear a small bark and someone yell something inaudible.

"Oh! Hi!" Tessa's dark hair is piled in a messy bun on the top of her head. Her arms are exposed to me for the first time, showing off sleeves of tattoos. She's wearing an oversized T-shirt with a stack of books that says *Get Lit.*

"I…uh…made you guys a lasagna." I smile, holding it out.

"You did?" Her face relaxes, features shifting from surprise to curiosity.

"Yeah, it's actually pretty hot; it just came out of the oven, if you don't mind…"

"Oh my goodness, of course!" Tessa opens the door completely, and I stomp my feet on the mat so I don't bring in any snow.

I follow her to the kitchen, my eyes on her ass. She's wearing these incredibly short shorts that make it so I can almost see the bottom of her ass as she walks. It's an amazing kind of torture. When she turns, I can see her nipples poking through her shirt. Her breasts hang low, and her nipples are hard as rocks. I swallow hard, trying to avert my gaze.

"Mommy!" Drew stumbles in from the back door, dropping his wet gloves on the floor by the door and swiping his dark curls out of his eyes.

"Wait! Rumi!" Tessa calls and sighs as the small golden puppy hops up and tries to sniff my leg.

"Rumi? From *KPop Demon Hunters*?" I ask, placing the lasagna pan on the counter.

"Yes, it's my favorite movie." Natalie smiles proudly.

"Such a good soundtrack." I nod. She looks at me curiously. Maybe it's weird for me to know a kid's movie, but the music does slap.

"Can you stay for dinner?" Tessa asks as she pulls plates from the cabinet.

"Not tonight, but rain check? I just wanted to make sure you guys had a hot meal when you got home." I smile. I want to stay, but I also want her to know this isn't some sneaky way of inserting myself into their dinner plans.

"Of course! Thank you so much." Tessa grins. "Kids, go wash your hands."

Natalie and Drew take off down the hall with Rumi chasing after them. Tessa leads me to the front door.

"You really didn't have to do this, you know." Tessa sighs. "My answer is still no."

"Hey, I didn't even ask you anything." I wink.

"Parker…" Tessa says.

"I know, but really. It's just about making sure you and the kids have a hot meal. I know it can be tough cooking every night after work. I'm not even asking you anything this time."

"Okay." She nods. "Thank you. It really does take a load off for me." Tessa finally looks relaxed. Relaxed and gorgeous. With those barely there pajamas and sexy tattoos.

"Just get me back the pan whenever? No rush, but I'll need it back for next time I cook for you." I wink.

"This doesn't have to be a thing."

"I know. Oh!" I remember the allergen info and pull the labels out of my pocket. "These are the labels of the ingredients I used. I just wanted to cover all my bases in case anyone has any allergies," I say, handing her the labels.

"Really?" Tessa looks them over. "That's so thoughtful. I really appreciate it. We're only allergic to pollen, so the springtime sucks, but we're okay with food."

"Awesome, good to know." I smile and head out the door.

I feel Tessa's gaze on me as I walk away. She doesn't shut the door completely until I'm halfway up my porch steps. I feel a sense of relief, knowing I did something to help her. The kids looked excited about the food, and Tessa looked relieved that she didn't have to cook after a long day. I'm happy knowing, even if this doesn't turn into anything, I've made her life a little easier tonight.

I really did want to stay tonight, but I didn't want to impose. Inviting myself over for dinner isn't the best way to get her to relax. I chuckle as I think about how mad my mother would get if someone came over unannounced after she took her bra off. If Tessa is the same way, then I definitely interrupted her relaxation time.

But God damn. Tessa is walking sex appeal. Her tattoos make

her even sexier. Who knew she was hiding all that under those winter coats and pants? I want to see where else she has tattoos —and what else she's hiding. This woman is slowly going to kill me. Even if I try to stay away, I know it's a losing battle. I need to find a way to get this woman to be mine…one way or another.

FIVE

Tessa

The weekends are my only days off, but I'm spending it unpacking the house and putting up holiday decorations. The kids were supposed to see their dad, but of course something came up at the last minute. I tried to hide my distaste and frustration and let them have their feelings. I don't ever want to influence them to feel any way about their dad, especially now. Both kids retreated to their rooms and are doing their own thing.

Last I checked on Drew, he had fallen asleep while building something with his Legos on the floor in his bedroom. It's adorable when that happens. I choose not to move him, knowing he'll wake up if I try.

Natalie is in her bedroom with her headphones on, listening to music and tuning out the world. She said she was fine when I asked about her dad not coming. She always says she's fine—that's about the most I get out of her. Talking to teenagers is rough.

I'm cleaning up the kitchen from brunch when I spot Parker's lasagna pan sitting in the sink. I let it soak it overnight to get the melted cheese and sauce off the pan easier. Now that I've washed it thoroughly, I can bring it over to her. I still can't believe she cooked us dinner. I also can't believe how delicious it tastes. Drew and Natalie both asked for seconds, that's how good it was.

I half anticipated her staying for dinner when she came over, but I was pleasantly surprised that she didn't. Not that I didn't want her to stay, I just didn't want to be ambushed. When she happily insisted on another time, it was clear her intention was pure. She genuinely just wanted to make sure we had dinner and to give me a night off from cooking. I can't remember the last time someone was so thoughtful without expecting anything in return.

Grabbing the pan, I walk back to Natalie's bedroom and knock on the door. I have to knock pretty loud so she hears, but she eventually gives me permission to come in.

"Hey, I'm going next door to return this okay?" I say.

"Okay." She nods and puts her earbuds back in.

I put on my winter gear and trudge across the snowy path to Parker's house. As I walk, I notice one of the lights is out in the string of lights I put up last week. I'll have to remember to fix that when I get back. I check to see if Parker's car is in the garage, and it is, so I knock twice on her door.

"Hey," Parker opens the door in a pair of Christmas pajama bottoms and a red tank top. Her red hair is wet, hanging down over her shoulders and on her chest.

"Hey, I just wanted to return this and say thank you." I hand her the pan.

"Oh, thanks. Do you want to come in? It's freezing and my hair..." She motions toward her wet strands.

"Uh, sure." I glance back at my house. It isn't like I'm going to be far, and Natalie knows where I am.

"Did it taste okay? Did the kids like it?" Parker asks, leading me into her house.

I take a moment to look around. It has a completely different layout than mine, but it's just as amazing. I love how modern all her furniture is. Her home smells amazing—maybe it's a candle or something, but it smells like hot chocolate and peppermint. It gives the place a cozy, lived-in feel. It isn't exactly what I expect from a single woman's house. It feels homier than mine currently does.

"They loved it; you'll have to give me the recipe sometime." I smile.

"Or I'll just make it again. Let me know when, and I'll be happy to." She bats her eyelashes at me, and for a moment, my gaze drops to her pretty pink lips. I don't know if it's lipstick or if that's her natural color, but I'm thinking about finding out.

"You don't have to do that," I say instead, clearing my throat.

"I think you'd be surprised by the free time you might have if you let others help you," Parker says. I grit my teeth; letting others help me has always been a problem for me. "I can see that won't be easy for you," she adds with a laugh.

"I just think I should be able to do it by myself," I admit.

"Who's saying you can't do it yourself? I'm just saying you don't *have* to." She smiles with a light shrug.

"Anyway, thank you for dinner. We will definitely return the favor once we're finally moved in," I say.

"I can't wait." Parker leads me back out, and I instantly miss the warmth her home has.

Heading back to my house, I notice the light again, so I head straight for the ladder on the back porch. I don't have a permanent spot for it yet, and I've been using it a lot lately—mainly to hang decorations outside. I grab the extra lightbulbs from inside and then set up the ladder, climb up to the second step, and reach for the lights. I have to detach them from the hook they're on and unscrew the small, unlit bulb. I place the bad one in my pocket and reach for the new one.

As I do, it slips from my gloved hands, and I reach out to catch it. Somehow my foot slips, and I go falling in slow motion. It's the slowest and fastest I've ever fallen in my entire life. I somehow have time to think about all the ways I'm going to get hurt—but there's still not enough time to catch myself from falling.

"Son of a bitch!" I shout as my body connects with the ground. My arm hits the hard porch, and I scream out in pain. It's blinding as I see stars for just a moment, and I'm grateful I didn't hit my head. I lie on the cold porch for what feels like forever before Natalie runs out of the house.

"Oh, shit! Mom?!" Natalie rushes to my side.

"D-don't curse," I mutter under my breath.

"Are you okay? Can you get up?" Natalie's trying to help me up as I hear footsteps running up our porch.

"What happened? Are you okay?" Parker's voice calms me. I'm trying not to scream and scare Natalie any more than I probably already have. Tears are pouring down my cheeks, and there's no doubt my arm is broken.

"I fell off the ladder. My arm hurts too much to move," I choke out.

"Okay." Parker pauses. "Natalie go get your brother and the keys to your mom's car so we can all go together. Tess, I can call you an ambulance, but I guarantee I can get us there faster—and I know all the cops in this town, I promise we won't get in trouble. Can you walk?"

"Okay. Yes. I can. It's just my arm, so I need help getting up." I nod.

Natalie looks at me, waiting for a confirmation before listening to a stranger. Then she runs inside, and Parker curls her arm around my waist to help me up. I hate feeling so helpless, but even this is killing me. There is no way I could get up on my own. Plus, she's right, I doubt the kids could come with me in the ambulance. This way at least we're all in the same car.

"Mom?" Drew rubs his eyes as Natalie zips up his coat.

"It's okay honey. I just got a bad boo boo, so we're going to see a doctor." I force a smile, trying not to worry him.

Parker walks me to the car and helps me in, even reaching over my body to buckle me in. I know it isn't the time, but god, she even smells good. Parker makes sure Natalie and Drew are buckled in before taking off. She's driving fast, but not like *Fast and the Furious* fast. She pulls right up to the emergency room entrance and helps me out.

"Sit here. I'll get you some help," Parker says, helping me sit in one of the empty chairs inside.

Drew and Natalie quietly sit by my side, waiting for further instructions. I try to smile to give them a little encouragement, but I'm running on fumes. It's taking everything inside of me to stay calm. I'm in so much pain. I've never broken anything before, but I can tell from the blinding pain that isn't going away that something is seriously wrong.

"Tessa? Can I have your last name for the forms?" a nurse asks. She's at least fifteen years younger than me and has dark black hair and dark skin.

"Williams. I have my ID in my wallet, if that's helpful."

"Yes, we got some information from your neighbor, but there are some blanks we need filled in before we can admit you." She smiles.

"It's in my front pocket." I look at Natalie, and she reaches into my coat to get it. She hands it to the nurse, who heads back to her desk and finishes filling out the forms.

"Miss Williams, you can come with us," a man in says a few minutes later.

"My kids—"

"I've got them," Parker says, appearing next to me.

"Are you sure?" I ask hesitantly. It isn't like she's going to run off with them. They're safer with Parker than sitting alone in the waiting room.

"Yes, just go get your arm looked at," Parker says and Natalie nods. Drew sits up straight and tries to be brave for me, but I know my son well enough to see through the act—he's nervous. Parker takes my seat, and I follow the man through the double doors. He helps me take off my jacket and layers, each movement met with additional pain. At least I don't have to hold back how shitty this feels anymore. I'm given a heavy dose of Tylenol for the pain, and then they take me for an X-ray.

"So you didn't break it, but you do have a mild fracture here. You'll need a thin cast and splint for at least the next several weeks. We'll have you follow up with your primary care doctor in a few weeks for follow up X-rays," the doctor explains, pointing at the X-ray of my arm on the screen.

"Am I able to work?" I ask anxiously.

"What do you do exactly?"

"I work in a library. It's mostly clerical work," I explain.

"Then, yes. I wouldn't do any heavy lifting or climb ladders anytime soon. But you should be fine to work. That's your dominant hand, correct? I wouldn't recommend driving for the next few weeks. It might be too much strain on that side," he continues.

Great. There goes my method of getting to work. Of course I had to fall on my right arm. I mean, what are the fucking odds? At least I can work, but how am I going to get there? It isn't like this town has Uber or Lyft. And I don't know anyone who I can carpool with. Is there even a bus in this town? I seriously doubt it.

"It's hard, but it helps if you have people you can count on. This is the time to ask for help," the doctor says before signing my discharge papers.

Of fucking course. Asking for help is the last thing I want to do. My family is back in Massachusetts, and I barely know anyone here. Who am I supposed to ask for help? Parker? No. I'll figure out a way to make this work. I need to figure out a way to make this work. My kids need to know they can count on me no matter what.

SIX

Parker

"Mom? How are you?" Natalie jumps up the moment she sees her mom walk out of the ER doors.

Tessa looks disheveled, but okay. Her dark hair is a mess around her face, hair coming out of her bun, and she's got a cast on her right arm that's held up by a black sling. I can't hear what they're saying, but Drew is quiet as he approaches his mom. He walks over to her cautiously, almost like he's afraid of her—or afraid of hurting her.

"Do you mind driving us home? I won't be driving for a bit," Tessa says with a nervous chuckle. I know she doesn't like asking for help, so this can't be easy for her.

"Of course. Do you need anything on the way home?" I ask.

"I could really go for a good burger. Maybe we can get some take out on the way?" she says with a laugh.

"McDonald's?" Drew asks hopefully.

"The closest one is forty-five minutes away." Natalie frowns while looking at her phone.

"What about Liz's diner? It's right in town, and I can call it in from the road," I suggest.

"Sounds perfect." Tessa smiles.

Natalie helps her mom walk to the car, even though she doesn't really need it. I can tell it's her way of helping. Both of her kids were terrified. I wonder if it made them realize their mother is human and capable of being hurt. Kids always think their parents are superheros until something makes them realize they aren't.

We call the diner on the way, and the kids shout out their orders while the phone is on speaker. I add a turkey club and onion rings for myself, and when we arrive, I run in to get it.

"This all for you Parker? You having the girls over or something?" Kate asks as I pay for the food. Tessa tried to give me money, but I used the fact that she couldn't reach her wallet with her to my advantage.

"Helping out my neighbor and her kids." Kate means well, but it's a small town, and I don't need the entire town gossiping about me. Let them form their own conclusions.

Back in the car, I place the food in the trunk and we head back to our street. Natalie carries in the food after helping her brother out of his car seat, and I help Tessa in. She denies needing help, but I insist because she doesn't need to slip in the snow on top of everything else she's now dealing with.

"Do you want to stay for dinner? You know, since you paid, and it's not like I can kick you out anyway," Tessa jokes.

"Mom! I'm letting Rumi out!" Natalie calls, and we hear a door open before a few happy barks echo in the space.

"I'll stay and then see if you need help with anything else after dinner," I suggest.

"I should be fine. We can handle our bedtime routine," she insists.

"And what about work on Monday? Do you have a way to get there? Or did the doctor say to take off?" I ask.

"He said I can work since it's nothing strenuous, but I can figure out the bus or—"

"This is a very small town Tess. We don't have a bus. And the train only brings you into the city or to other towns," I say, cutting her off.

"Oh." She sighs.

"I don't mind giving you a ride to work in the morning," I suggest.

"No, no—"

"I know you don't want to ask for help," I say, cutting her off again. "But you're not asking, I'm offering, and I'll back off if you have another way to get yourself to work. But I'm pretty sure, unless you want Natalie driving you, I'm your best option."

Tessa stares at me, contemplating her answer before sighing. "You're right. Yes, I would love a ride. Is seven thirty too early? I have to be there before eight to open up."

"Not at all," I lie. That'll be the earliest I've woken up in years…except for when I was fighting for my life for Olivia Rodrigo concert tickets. But I don't want Tessa to feel like it's an issue.

"Thank you." She sighs. I can see this is hard on her, but I'm hoping the extra time together will give her a chance to warm up to the idea of going out with me.

"What time do you get out of work?" I ask.

"Oh, I'm usually done around 4:30 or 5:00. Is that too late? I can probably find—"

"I'm done with work until the new year, so I'm happy driving you and picking you up. Where's your phone? Let me put my number in so you can shoot me a text when you're almost done with work," I suggest.

"Okay." Tessa reaches for her phone in her pocket and hands it to me unlocked. I add my phone number and send myself a text so I know her number too.

"Mom! The food's getting cold!" Natalie calls, and we join them at the kitchen table.

Natalie's placed everyone's food in front of their seats and grabbed glasses of water for everyone too. She seems to be used to getting things together. Drew is already digging in to his chicken fingers, and Tess is looking at her burger. I never really thought about it before, but a burger is usually something you use both hands to eat. Rumi's on the floor, near her dog bowl, eating her dinner. Her little tail wags as she drops the kibble on the tile floor.

"I guess I should've ordered something else." Tessa laughs.

"You could cut it in half?" Natalie suggests.

"Good idea." Tessa smiles and Natalie helps her mom cut her food. "It seems like just yesterday I was cutting up your food for you."

"Moooom," Natalie groans.

"I know, I know." She smiles.

Tessa kisses the top of Natalie's head and picks up one half of her burger. She groans as she eats it, and my cheeks heat up. I've never heard her make a sound like that, but fuck, I want to hear it again. I bite the inside of my cheek and pick up another onion ring. She's just eating—there's nothing sexual about it. But as Tessa takes another bite, she moans and closes her eyes in pleasure. I gulp. Yup, definitely nothing sexual about that. Too bad I can't convince the heat between my thighs of that. I'll be thinking about it when I'm home alone later.

"Everything okay?" Tessa asks, and I realize I've missed something.

"Oh, yes." I clear my throat. "Just great food."

"It really is, I'm glad you recommended it." Tessa smiles. She touches my arm, and I feel a shiver shoot down my spine. Tess gives it a slight squeeze, and I lock eyes with her. Her red lips are bare tonight, gone is the usual lipstick she wears. I smile at her, and she gives me a quick smirk before moving her hand and using it to eat.

"I should get going, but I'll see you Monday. Let me know if you need help with anything before then."

"That sounds great. Seriously, thank you again," Tessa says, walking me out. Rumi follows us, looking at me happily, her tail swinging back and forth.

I head out the front door and down the path that connects our houses. It's surprisingly not snowing, so there's no shoveling that needs to be done. I decide to grab a beer and take a shower upstairs. It's not something I've ever done, but taking an ice-cold beer into a steaming-hot shower might just be my new destressing routine. I'm rinsing off the day, the hospital germs, and everything else. It's dark out by the time I get out of the shower. One of the downfalls of winter is the sun setting before five o'clock. I head back downstairs with my phone and lie on the couch. I turn on *Home Alone*, in need of a little Christmas nostalgia tonight.

I yawn as I hear my phone alerting me of a Ring notification. I must've fallen asleep because now I'm halfway through *Home Alone 2*, and I don't even remember starting that one. I sit up, look at my phone, and see it's a notification for my back door. It'll usually alert me for the occasional bear, but this doesn't look like a bear. I laugh to myself as I realize what's climbing over my backyard fence. Heading to the back door, I flip on the porch lights just as it reaches the middle of my yard. Like a deer in headlights, it attempts to flee, but I've caught it.

"You're joking, right?" I say just loud enough for Natalie to hear me.

She's dressed in a mini skirt any mother would have a fit over and a pair of boots—no jacket. In her hands are a pair of heels that I'm sure are not hers. She looks at me like she isn't sure what her next move should be. Apparently she didn't expect to get caught.

"Get your ass over here." I wave her over and she runs to the porch, shivering.

"Yes?"

I laugh—this girl has balls. "*Yes?* Dude, you've got to be kidding me. Your mom doesn't need this right now. Where are you even going?"

Natalie looks at me like she isn't sure if she should trust me.

"Every house on this block has Ring cameras in the front and back of their houses. So if you think there's anywhere for you to go except home, you're mistaken," I explain.

Natalie sighs. "I was going to the train station."

"And how did you plan to get there? You realize it's, like, a two-mile walk."

"What? It said it was twenty minutes!" She looks at her phone as if Apple Maps has betrayed her.

"Maybe if the town wasn't covered in snow? And you have to pass the woods, which I wouldn't recommend if you'd like to avoid being eaten by bears." I shrug.

"Fuck." She sighs.

"I'll let that one slide, but do you wanna tell me where you planned on going once you got to the train station?" Natalie looks at me hesitantly. "I can keep a secret if that's what you're worried about."

"Fine. I was going to meet my friends in Boston. I was supposed to go there this weekend—to my dad's house. But he didn't come, so I couldn't see my friends." She sighs again.

"That sucks." Her head snaps up, like she hadn't anticipated me saying that. "It must be hard being so far from your dad and your friends, especially around the holidays."

"It is." She nods.

"Have you talked to your mom about this?"

"She wouldn't understand." She shakes her head.

"You'd be surprised. My mom was a single parent like your mom, and I know it's not easy when things change, but your mom might understand more than you think she will." She shrugs, so I take that as a win. "I'm going to give you the chance to sneak back in, and as long as you stay in, I won't tell your mom about this. She has enough going on. But seriously, talking to her about it might be easier than jumping state lines."

"Yeah, okay," she grumbles.

"Come on. I'll show you where the side gate is." I slip on my boots that I leave by the back door and unlock the side gate for her. She goes back to her side of the fence, and I wait until I hear her window shut before going back inside.

I should probably tell Tessa about this, but I decide to give Natalie a break. At least for tonight. She's home safe, and she's probably just missing her friends. She won't be able to get into too much trouble here, considering everyone's business is just that...

Everyone's business.

SEVEN

Tessa

Every year Natalie, Drew, and I make gingerbread houses and decorate them to look like a little town. We usually bake them from scratch, but with the move this year, I wasn't sure we'd have enough time to bake them. So, thankfully I bought five store-bought sets of houses. Three of the boxes have only one house, and the other two have sets of three smaller houses. have extra candy, frosting, and, of course, our special secret for gluing them together—sugar that I cooked and am keeping hot. I have everything out and ready by the time Drew and Natalie wake up. Rumi's even had breakfast and been outside twice, so she's resting in the corner now.

"What's all this?" Natalie asks, looking around.

"It's time to build our gingerbread town." I smile.

"We're really still doing this?" She scoffs.

"Yes, I think it will be fun." I force myself to stay positive.

"I want this one!" Drew calls from the table. He's already opening one of the boxes and pulling the candy out of the plastic.

"Fine, but I get the little ones." Natalie lets out a long breath. When it comes to family activities, she hates disappointing her little brother.

We all sit down, and I turn on the speaker on the kitchen island to play popular Christmas hits. Drew is shaking his little butt, unable to sit still while he's figuring out how to put together the house. I help him with the sugar, since it's pretty hot, but it works like glue and dries just as quick. Then we're all able to decorate our houses.

"I'm going to make mine look like the OVERWORLD in Minecraft!" Drew says excitedly.

"I think I'm going to decorate mine for Christmas." I smile.

"You always do that, mommy," Drew complains.

"I'm going to make it look like the scars from *KPop Demon Hunters*," Natalie says.

"Ooo, that's cool," Drew and I say in unison.

"What do you think about this?" She turns her house around and shows Drew.

"It needs more candy." He giggles while stealing one of the Skittles from her plate.

Natalie laughs and I relax. It's so nice to have a family moment like this. I've been a little afraid that things wouldn't be like this anymore, but I feel like it might even be better than it used to be. In the past, Weston would be in the background, giving us a hard time for being too loud or having too much fun. He didn't like getting his hands sticky, so he never wanted to join. After a while, we started doing things like this while he was at work so we didn't have to hear his comments.

"Do you think Dad's coming next weekend?" Natalie asks.

"I honestly don't know." I sigh. "He's supposed to, but I can't promise anything."

"I miss Daddy." Drew frowns. God, I wish I knew how to make their father show up for his children. He's making everything harder than it needs to be—especially on them.

"Do you think if Dad doesn't come, we could still take a trip home—I mean, to Boston?" Natalie asks.

"I don't know…it's a long drive, and I'm not actually supposed to do that right now." I frown.

"Oh." Natalie's face falls. "I just really miss my friends. It's been hard without them."

Natalie isn't usually one to open up to me like this, so I tread with caution. "I understand, maybe we can see if your grandma is around to pick you up, and you can plan something with your friends that way? Maybe for the New Year?" I suggest.

"Really?" Her eyes light up.

"Can I see grandma too?" Drew asks happily.

"I don't see why not. I'll give her a call later and hash out the details." I smile.

"Thanks, Mom! You're the best!" Natalie jumps up and wraps her arms around me. I try not to wince when she hugs my neck a little too tightly.

"I'm glad you told me how you're feeling. I know all these changes aren't easy on you kids so if there are things I can do to make it easier, I'm happy to talk about it," I say.

"I was worried you wouldn't understand," Natalie admits, sitting back down.

"I'll always try my best to."

"I bet my house would withstand any zombie creepers attacking, but yours looks like it came out of a Hallmark movie." Drew teases.

"It's *Hallmark*, little bro. If you're going to insult someone, make sure you say the name right." She laughs.

It's seven twenty-five a.m., and I'm hauling ass to get everyone ready. Drew is being especially cranky this morning and only just got out of bed. Natalie is sitting on the couch scrolling on her phone but refuses to help, since she's "doing the most" by being awake. I don't blame her—we all had a rough weekend. Rumi is knocking on the back door, waiting to come in. I've already filled her bowl, so she should be good until we get home. I finish helping Drew get dressed and grab our lunch boxes from the kitchen counter along with my coffee. Somehow, I'm able to juggle everything with my good arm, and Natalie opens the front door for me.

"Good morning." Natalie smiles at Parker, who's standing outside our front door with her arm extended.

"Good morning. Are we late? I'm sorry." I sigh.

"Nope. Right on time." She slides her phone in her jacket pocket and takes the lunch boxes from me. "Keys?"

"Oh, yes." I grab the car keys off the hook and hand them to Parker.

The kids head to the car first, giving me a moment to take in Parker. Somehow it's before eight a.m., and she looks like a God damn model. Her red hair is perfectly straight under a white winter hat, and her black coat is hugging her middle. Her nails are painted with little candy canes on them, and her makeup is completely done. I threw my makeup bag in my work bag, hoping I had the chance to do it when I got to work. Since she has the keys, she locks the door behind us and helps me with the door to the car. Natalie helps Drew buckle up, and Parker is the last one in.

"All set?" She looks back at the kids and then to me.

"Yes, thank you again." I smile. Lifting my coffee cup to my lips, I take a sip of the hot mocha I made.

"Don't worry about it. What are neighbors for?" She winks and I melt a little bit into the seat. I hate that she has this effect over me.

"If you can't pick us—"

"I already told you I can; it's not a problem." She reaches over and squeezes my thigh gently. I tense and my breathing nearly stops. I haven't had someone touch me there in a long time. It wasn't even sexual, I mean, my kids are in the backseat, and it only lasted a second. But my center is on fire, and I can't think straight.

"Sorry. I wasn't thinking," Parker whispers quietly.

"It's okay," I whisper back and take a long sip of coffee while I look out the cold window.

I don't have time to even think about Parker like this right now. My life is a mess, and although she's been helpful lately, I know she doesn't want to sign up for this permanently. When we pull up to the library, Parker helps me with the keys to the door.

"Just shoot me a text when you're almost done. It's only a fifteen-minute drive over." She smiles.

"Thank you." I smile and she nods.

"Come on kids."

The library opens in thirty minutes, and I have a few things to do first. We get Drew setup in the kid's section, and he starts playing with Legos as Natalie helps me turn on all the computers and open the blinds. Paige is the next one in, but she walks in with a few patrons. I unlock the bathrooms and then head to my office.

"We're taking the Legos to the rec room. Paige said it's okay!" Natalie calls with Drew on her way back.

"Okay! Have fun!" I take their lunch boxes to the break room fridge and find Paige hanging up her coat.

"Hey, good morning," she says cheerfully. "Whoa what happened?" she asks, spotting my arm.

"Good morning," I say as chipper as I can. "I fell off a ladder while hanging Christmas lights. It's broken, but I'm alright."

"Shit! I'm so sorry. If you need help with anything today just let me know. Mondays are usually slow, and I'm happy to help," Paige says.

"Thanks." I smile.

I'm not going to take her up on her offer. I don't want to be relying on anyone else through this. I still have to call my mom and see if she can take the kids this weekend. I head back to my office and call her, but she doesn't pick up so I send her a text instead.

• • •

ME: Are you free this weekend? Could you watch the kids? And maybe come get them? I broke my arm and they want to see you.

I'm laying it on a little thick, but truthfully, I need a break. It's going to take me twice as long to get through everything I need to do for the house. And it will go a lot easier if I don't have my little helpers around. Besides, what are grandparents for if not to take the kids they begged you to have off your hands? Almost instantly, my mom calls me back.

"Are you okay? Why didn't you tell us you broke your arm? Do you need me to come down today?" Her voice is full of worry, just like I expected it to be.

"I'm fine, really. But Weston didn't take the kids last weekend and they were upset. Drew was hoping to spend some time with you and Natalie really needs some time with her friends. The move has been hard on her." I sigh.

"Of course. We can come down Friday by noon. Will you be at work? We can stop there and grab you for a quick lunch," she says hopefully.

"I can't really leave work for too long, but yes, the kids will be with me."

"How have you been getting to work if you can't drive?" she asks. I hoped she wouldn't pick up on that.

"Our new neighbor has been driving us. Well, today was the first day," I admit.

"Oh, honey. You really shouldn't bother your neighbors with stuff like that. They probably have enough on their plate, and you shouldn't ask them for that." she scolds me, which only serves to remind me where my hatred for asking for help comes from. She's always been quick to tell me—throughout my entire life—that asking for help is like admitting defeat.

"She works from home and doesn't mind, Mom. Plus, I didn't have many options. There aren't Uber or bus service out here." I roll my eyes. Maybe she's right about asking Parker for help.

"Then you should've called me..."

"You have enough going on with the holiday parade in town and the choir group," I remind her. This time of year is always particularly busy for her, which is why I didn't call her earlier.

"You're right. I wouldn't have anyone to lead the meetings, and you know they're a disaster without me." I can picture her frowning on the other end of the phone. She keeps her dark hair dyed to match mine, and she has a few wrinkles around the corners of her eyes and cheekbones.

"So you can get them Friday? I have to get back to work, but we can chat more later," I say, although I'm really not too busy. I just want to get off the phone.

"Yes, tell Natalie to text me anything she wants to eat," my mom says cheerfully, and we say our goodbyes.

EIGHT

Parker

The first three days of picking up Tessa and the kids goes easier than I anticipated. The kids are nice, even Natalie smiles at me now. I think she's worried I'm going to tell her mom about her failed mission to sneak out. But since I haven't seen her trying to do it again, I don't see why I need to. Like I had told Natalie, Tessa has enough on her plate. But on Wednesday afternoon, I notice Tessa's in a bad mood. Her whole demeanor is different; it's like she's a deflated balloon.

"What's wrong?" I ask as Tessa gets in the car.

"I wanted to decorate for the holidays in the library, but because of my stupid arm, it's going to be impossible." She sighs.

"Well, it's decorated in the rec room for Jax's event." I smile. I'd explained to Tess how my best friend was in fear of losing her family's bookstore and will be using the library's rec room to host a holiday fundraiser.

"I know, but I had all these ideas and goals to do for this year when you walk into the library. I guess I'll have to wait to do them next year." She's scrolling on her phone on what looks like Pinterest. She swipes out of the app with a groan and puts her phone away.

"Everyone's seatbelts on?" I ask, looking at the backseat. I don't know what else I can say to comfort Tessa.

"Yes!" the kids say, and I drive us toward home.

Tessa's quiet today, but Drew is filling the silence with Minecraft facts. He's asking the car, but Natalie has her headphones in and Tessa is too deflated to feign a reply right now.

"I thought the green guys are called creepies," I tell Drew, who bursts out with laughter.

"No! They're called creepers! They explode and can blow up the whole house," Drew explains.

"Ohhh, what about the skeleton guys? What do they do?" I ask.

"They're usually in the Nether and can have bow and arrows to shoot people," he says.

"Hmm, what do you like the best?" I ask.

"The animals! There are cows, piggies, sheep…" Drew goes on naming animals as I drive. I only hear every other one, but I'm nodding along as he names them all.

"Thank you," Tessa whispers quietly and smiles at me. I nod slightly and smile back.

"We're home!" I announce as I pull into their driveway.

It snowed while they were at the library, but I shoveled a path for the car and then her porch, too. I don't want her attempting to do all of that with a broken arm, especially after a long day at work. I help Tessa out of the car while Natalie gets Drew out and unlocks the front door.

"Did you shovel?" Tessa asks, looking confused.

"Yeah, it snowed while you were at work." I shrug.

"You didn't have to do that."

"I know, but don't worry about it," I say.

"Thank you. I don't know how we'd survive this week without you. I'm sorry I was in such a sour mood today. I was just really looking forward to decorating. And I thought I missed it by getting this job so late, but then I didn't, and now I still can't do anything," Tessa explains.

I take a moment to take it all in. This is the first time she's really venting to me, so I don't want to say something stupid. "If you wanted hel—"

"No, thank you. I just needed to vent. I'm sure I'll have the opportunity to decorate next year." She shrugs.

I help her inside, and when I spot her car keys, I think about what I can do. They jingle as I swipe them off the key rack, and Tessa looks at me.

"I left my gloves in your car, do you mind?" I lie.

Tessa shakes her head, and I sneak back outside. In case she's looking, I pretend to grab gloves and fake putting them in my pocket. I'm actually just unhooking the key for the library from her key ring. Thankfully, she doesn't notice that I also grabbed her house key ring, which has the key to the library. I've seen her use it every morning to unlock the door, and it's labeled in case I wasn't sure. I put the keys back on the hook unnoticed and say goodbye.

The second I'm outside, I head for my car and call Jax's little sister, Paige.

"Parker? What's up?" She seems confused, which makes sense. I don't usually call her. Once in a while, we text, but that's usually only about Jax.

"Can you do me a favor and tell your boss I'll be stopping by the library? I have a key and don't want the cops called if you guys have a security system," I explain.

"Our security system doesn't work. We've been asking the town to fix it for years, and they don't care. But Dawn does have a Ring system set up by the front entrance to watch the comings and goings. Does this have to do with the rec room? Because there's a separate entrance for that," Paige explains.

"Can you keep a secret?" I sigh, this will only work if I can tell her the truth.

"Of course, unless it's about Jax, then I might spill. Depending on how juicy it is."

At least she's honest.

"I'm neighbors with your new employee, Tessa—"

Paige cuts me off with a squeal. "Oh my god! Isn't she the best? She's so sweet, and her kids are so cute!"

"Yes, so I stole the key so I could decorate the library for her. She was really looking forward to it, and now she can't because of her broken arm. I was hoping to get in there tonight and do it," I explain.

"Oh my goodness! Yes, this is so cute! I can't believe I didn't know about you two."

"We're not—I mean, maybe? It's complicated right now, but I'm trying to show her I'm an option," I say.

"Got it. Let me know if you need any help. I can swing by and help with anything you need," she offers.

"Really? I may need that," I admit.

"You got it. Is there a theme or something?" she asks.

"She said she had a lot of ideas on her Pinterest board, but I haven't been able to look at it yet."

"Okay, give me one second. Her last name is Williams right?"

"Uh, yes?" I struggle to remember, but then I think about her last name freshly stickered on the mailbox.

"Okay, here it is. Holy crap these are cool ideas! What if we use the discarded books to make the decorations? We should have the other supplies in the art cart," Paige says. "Would you be cool if I brought Sierra? She's incredible with anything artistic."

"If she wants to help, that would be amazing. I'm trying to pull this off overnight so she can be surprised tomorrow morning," I explain.

"Yes, the more the merrier then. I got it. I'm sending my boss a text right now so you can head right in. It's after hours, so do what you need," Paige says.

"Thank you so much."

I drive back to the library and head inside. It's weird being in here alone. It isn't spooky, necessarily, but I just keep waiting to run into someone and I never do. I pull up Tessa's Pinterest from a link Paige sent me and start scrolling. I save the things that I think are actually possible to do. There are a few that I can't imagine anyone doing, but I'm sure Tessa could surprise me.

Paige shows up with her roommate, Sierra, and a backseat full of supplies. "What did you do, rob a dollar store?" I ask.

"We had a lot of leftover decorations at our place, plus some new things we picked up on the way." Paige shrugs. "We also have a closet full of decorations we can use. And I texted Dawn, she knows we're here and said we can stay until whenever."

"Perfect, whenever you guys need to go, I completely understand. I appreciate any help at all," I say.

"No worries, we weren't doing anything tonight." Paige smiles.

Paige wasn't joking about Sierra's art skills. Apparently, she went to art school on scholarship—which is evident in the way she looks at photos and immediately knows how to execute them. She created a wreath of book pages from the discarded and damaged books Paige found under the circulation desk. Apparently if a book isn't checked out in over fifteen years, or if it's damaged beyond repair, they de-shelve it and use the pages for art projects. I like that they upcycle the books to give them a new life.

Paige and I take care of the easier projects—like collecting green books and creating a tree of books at the front of the library. We use actual decorations, like a star and colored ornaments to decorate it. It looks really cute, so we also gather books with a white spine and create a snowman on an empty shelf. We put on some black circles for buttons and a face and use books with a black spine for a hat. This is the most creative I've been in years, but all I can think about is the look on Tessa's face when she sees it tomorrow.

I don't think lights are a good idea with all the books. I don't know how safe holiday lights are, and I don't want to be responsible for accidentally burning down the entire library. But following Tessa's Pinterest board, she has a lot of ideas that don't involve lights. I use recycled paper to make a garland around the bookshelves. There are signs Paige grabs from the dollar store and lots of other decorations. I know it might not be exactly what Tessa is envisioning, but it's the thought that counts, right? I just know I hate seeing her so upset and not doing anything about it.

Paige and I put up snowflake and holiday window clings on all the windows. Sierra cuts out intricate snowflakes from the used books and makes a garland out of them. It's definitely turning out better than I anticipate with Sierra being here.

"Food's here!" I call as I meet the delivery boy at the library door. It's one of the teenagers Liz likes to hire at the diner.

I bought Paige and Sierra dinner as a huge thank you for helping tonight. It's almost midnight, and despite the place looking great, we're only half done. I had suggested food and ordered us Liz's diner—the only place open this late. I got a turkey burger and onion rings, continuing my trend of trying something new. For the longest time, I ordered the same thing every time I went: the chicken fingers and mozzarella stick combo. But at some point a few years ago, I decided to stop being boring and expand my palette. Which is why I'm ordering something different until I make my way completely through the menu.

"You must have it bad for this girl," Sierra comments as she eats her fries.

"I really do." I nod. There's no denying it.

Tessa is beautiful, smart, and an amazing mother. Her kids love her so much, and she always put them first. That seems like an obvious thing to do, but I've been around too many parents who think of their kids as an accessory rather than people. It's refreshing to meet a woman who isn't just dropping everything for a relationship.

Even if nothing happens between the two of us, at least it

won't be for lack of effort on my part. I don't want to leave any stone unturned. I'm showing her exactly what she can have if she decides to be with me. She'll never have to ask for help with me, because I'll be taking care of it before she can even ask. I don't even mind. I just want to be the one to do it. I just hope she'll eventually see that.

NINE

Tessa

Parker knocks on our door a few minutes late today, but I'm grateful for the extra time. She looks exhausted—like she was up all night or forgot to go to sleep. There's dark bags under her eyes. I wonder if she went out with someone. I know it shouldn't bother me, but the thought of her out with someone else puts knots in my stomach. I turned her down, so of course she's allowed to go out with someone else. But I guess I hoped her promise to get me to change my mind was real and not just some line. She opens the door for me and lets me lean on her so I can get in.

"Are you okay? You look tired," I say.

"I'm fine," She shrugs me off. She doesn't look disoriented or anything—just sleepy.

When we get to the library, we say goodbye, and I pull out my keys. My heart drops when I notice the key to the library is missing. "Crap, where's the key to the library?" I mumble, searching through my purse.

"Hey, you dropped this," Parker says as she walks up behind me. She's holding up the key to the library. I let out a huge sigh of relief.

"Thank you! I thought I lost it." She hands me the key and I unlock the door. She surprises me by coming in behind us.

"Whoa! Mom!" Drew shouts, and I look up, shocked.

"How…" I say quietly as I look around.

Drew and Natalie take off to look through the rest of the library, but I'm frozen in place. The library looks exactly like my Pinterest board. The tree of books, the wreath of book pages… holiday decorations everywhere. The book snowman. How did this happen? But then I look at the library key in my hand and glance at Parker—an exhausted Parker who just so happened to have the key.

"Did you do this?" My eyes water.

"Yeah, I mean I had a little help." Parker shrugs.

I drop the bags I'm holding and close the distance between us. I'm not denying this for even one second longer. I wrap my arm around Parker's neck, and our lips melt together. She pulls me in tightly, her arms on the small of my back as I wrap my free hand around the nape of her neck. My body touches hers, and it's like a million fireworks go off at once. Her tongue slips into my mouth, and I lose sight of everything else.

We pull back slightly, and her eyes meet mine. "Wow," she whispers.

"I can't believe you did all this for me." I don't know if I've ever felt so loved and understood.

"I knew it meant a lot to you." She smiles, her pink lips matching the pink hue on her cheeks.

"Mom!" Drew comes running, and we break apart.

"Yes?" I brush my lips as if there's some way he can tell we were just kissing.

"You gotta come see this!" He tugs on my hands, and I look back at Parker, but she urges me to go and follows closely behind.

"Someone made a fireplace out of books! Isn't that cool?" He shows me, and I admire it.

There was so much thought put into it—the books making a

shelf, the paper used creatively to look like fire, and the mantle above it. It's one of the things I had on my board that I wasn't even sure I could create, but it was so cute that I knew I wanted to try.

"Sierra, Paige's roommate, made that. I'm not bad with stickers on windows and stacking books, but no way am I that crafty." Parker laughs.

"Wow, this is so cool." I smile.

"Drew, come on, let's go put our stuff away." Natalie wrangles her excited brother, and I lead Parker to my office.

"I'm sorry for kissing you like that," I say, realizing how that might've looked.

"Why? I'm not." Parker smirks dangerously at me. Then it hits me: she wasn't exhausted from being up late with anyone; she was up late from creating this masterpiece for me.

"Let me take you on a proper date. Dinner and a show—or at least dinner. I think I've made it clear that I can fit in wherever you have room for me," Parker says, taking my hand.

"Okay." I nod.

"Yes?" Parker's face lights up.

"Yes." I smile, my face matching hers.

"Are you free tomorrow night?" she asks. "I'd say tonight, but I definitely need to catch up on my sleep."

"Tomorrow night is perfect." I smile.

Parker leans in for one last quick peck before the kids come back. "Tomorrow, then." Parker beams and then leaves, heading for home.

Natalie raises an eyebrow at me, "Yes?" I ask.

"Nothing, just haven't seen you smile like that in a long time. It's nice." She grins at me.

"Do me a favor and bring your brother to the Lego club at noon today, okay? There should be kids his age and maybe some who will be in his class," I say, changing the subject. I don't want to talk about anything with Natalie yet. I don't even know what's happening.

"Of course." Natalie nods.

The decorations and the kiss threw me off of my routine. I shake my head to clear my lust-induced fog and then pick up my lunch box and head to the kitchen. After placing it in the fridge, I stop at the circulation desk to pick up any notes or anything I missed yesterday. Paige is sitting at the desk, wearing a bright red Christmas sweater with bows all over it.

"Good morning!" she says cheerfully.

"Good morning, you sneaky little spy. I assume Dawn was also in on this decorating mission?" I guess, raising an eyebrow.

"Yes, I texted her last night so she wouldn't call the cops on your girlfriend." Paige winks and I blush.

"Is it that obvious?" I whisper.

"To anyone with eyes. It's the way she looks at you. Plus, I don't know any neighbor of mine who would go out of their way to do something like this." She gestures to the room full of decorations.

"I guess you're right. Just don't say anything to my kids. I don't want them involved until I figure out whatever *this* is," I explain.

"Of course. Your secret is safe with me." She moves her hand across her lips, making a zipping motion.

As I head back to my office, I look at Parker's attention to detail. Almost everywhere has some kind of decoration. Even if it's as small as snowflake window clings on a window, the place is fully decorated. Meeting and *falling* for Parker was the last thing I anticipated happening. I thought I'd have to let her down gently, but somehow she's been able to show me I might've been wrong. And maybe asking for help every once in a while isn't the worst thing.

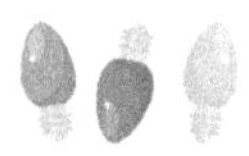

Friday morning at six a.m., I get a text from Weston. I'm still in bed, my alarm having just gone off, and I'm already pissed. Not even a phone call, but a stupid text about how he can't make it—again. His house isn't ready, so he and his new wife are spending the weekend at a hotel while the painters finish the kids' rooms. I'm shocked he even has rooms for the kids. I'm relieved that my mom is coming today, or else the kids would be even more let down than they were last week. At least they already planned on going to their grandma's house. I'm not trying to wreck their image of their father, but it's getting harder and harder with the way he's acting.

I don't bother replying. There's nothing I can say to him that I haven't said before, and nothing that will make any sort of difference. I wonder if I should've pushed harder for full custody in the divorce. He wanted shared, but I think it was more about maintaining his image. If he had shared custody with his ex-wife, he must *not* be a terrible father, right? In reality, Parker knows the kids better than he does now. And while I love that for me, it's a huge disappointment for the kids.

Speaking of Parker, tonight is our first date. Although I don't know what she has planned for us, I have an outfit ready. Hanging on the back of my bedroom door is my favorite red sweater dress. It hugs my curves and makes me look a few years years younger. That can't hurt, considering our obvious age difference. It's something we've never addressed, so I assume it isn't something she's worried about.

I didn't know exactly how old she is until I did a simple Google search last week. If she was going to be driving me and my kids around, I wanted to make sure she wasn't some kind of criminal with a record. Thankfully, all I learned was her age, which isn't surprising, considering how young she looks. She's at least twenty-seven, according to what I found, which is a bit away from my forty-two. I know there are couples out there with larger age differences, so I try not to let it bother me too much.

I get the kids ready in a rush. They're all packed for my

mom's house. I gave Natalie a key to give to Grandma when she comes to get them, that way they can stop at the house and pick up their bags. It's only two nights, but Natalie has at least four bags packed. Something about being prepared for every outfit possibility. When I kissed her good morning, she was buzzing with excitement about getting to see her friends again.

"Your location is still on, right?" I ask Natalie.

"Yes. Tonight is the sleepover at Amelia's house, and then tomorrow we're not sure what we're doing. But I'll make sure to text you and Grandma with updates." She smiles.

"Perfect, thank you." I relax a bit. I know she's responsible, but she's also thirteen. It doesn't hurt to have the added protection of knowing where she's going and who she's with.

"Parker's here!" Drew announces as he tosses his cereal bowl in the sink. The spoon clinks against the side of the sink, and I rinse the bowl with water so the milk won't smell.

"Good morning." Parker smiles as she stands in the doorway, covered in snow. Her boots are making wet marks on the welcome mat.

"Did it snow already?" I sigh.

"Yes. But don't worry, I got your car cleaned off." She smiles and I relax. "All good for later?" she asks quietly while the kids are getting their shoes on.

"Yes. I'm looking forward to it." I smile.

"Good." The tension hangs in the air between us for a moment.

I want to lean in and kiss her pink lips, but my kids could be back any second. I can tell she's thinking about kissing me, too, because her eyes haven't left my lips since she walked in. A shiver runs down my spine, and I force myself to focus on getting us out of the house on time. I slip on my boots and call for Natalie and Drew. Both come running, and we pile into the car.

As Parker drives, I admire her face. All her red hair is pulled into her knitted hat today, and she's barely wearing any makeup.

Her cheeks are bright pink from the cold, matching the only makeup she's wearing on her lips. She glances over at me as she drives and smiles. The way we keep stealing stolen glances at each other make me feel like a teenager hiding from my parents. Of course Drew and Natalie are oblivious—both in their own worlds. It just makes it easier to fantasize about being with her later.

TEN

Parker

"You still won't tell me where we're going?" Tessa laughs as she gets into my car. It's a little smaller than hers, and there aren't any car seats in the back.

"There aren't too many choices in town, so I thought we'd go to the next town over and grab dinner. Then, if you're up for it, the elementary school is putting on their holiday play," I explain.

"You're taking me to a kids play?" She raises an eyebrow.

"Or not? It's kind of cute, they sing songs, and the whole town usually goes. It's more of a community thing," I say.

"No, no, it's cute." She nods.

The second she opened her front door, I knew I was in for a night. She's wearing this gorgeous red dress that tightly touches every inch of her body. I gulped and reminded myself not to just invite her in before the date started. This is a woman who needs romance in her life—not a sleazy one night stand. No matter how much I want to see that dress on my bedroom floor. I squeeze my thighs together and clear my throat. Is it getting hot in here?

"So the kids are with your mom?" I ask, changing the subject.

"Yes, they were supposed to be with their dad but..." She shrugs.

"Well, I'm sure they'll have fun."

"Oh, yes. My mother is the queen of fun. There are no rules for them at her house. I'll be lucky if she doesn't give them sugar for every meal." Tessa laughs.

"Was it like that for you growing up?"

"Not so much. My mother was sterner. Not strict, but there was a lot of expected self-sufficiency." She sighs.

"Is that where you get it from then? Not being able to ask for help?"

"Oh, yes. It's something I didn't even notice until you pointed it out. But I think I'm getting better with it." She smiles.

"I think so too." I nod as we pull into the restaurant.

I shut off the car and race to the other side to open the door for her. Truth be told, I know she doesn't need my help with opening the door or walking. But I like being able to open the door for her. The place is fancier than I expected, but they seat us at a booth in the back with low lighting. We look over the menu, and I want to try everything. It all sounds as good as it looked on their social media.

"What do you say we split the mac and cheese bites?" I ask, leaning over my menu.

"Oooh yes. I was torn between those or the grilled salmon for dinner." She nods and puts the menu down.

"Anything to drink?" the waiter asks, placing down coasters for our drinks.

"A glass of chardonnay?" Tessa says.

"Make that two." I add. "And we'll have the mac and cheese bites to start."

"Perfect, I'll get those right away." The waiter smiles.

Tessa rolls up her sleeve, and it's the first time I'm able to actually appreciate the art on her arm. I look at the stack of books she has running down the side of her left arm, with titles written on the spine of each book. There's an array of leaves, trees, and mountains next to the stack of books. Her left is still covered by the cast; she seems to forgo the sling most days.

"Do you have any tattoos?" Tessa asks, catching my attention.

"I don't." I shake my head. "I want one, but I can never commit to one idea. I'm always changing my mind," I admit.

"I get that. I never get a tattoo without thinking about it for a long time, and that works most of the time."

"Most of the time?" I ask.

"Well, there is one tattoo I absolutely hated and had to cover up." She pulls the V-neck of her dress down, showing me the side of her left collarbone. There's an array of beautiful multicolored flowers I can only see the tops of. "It was this really terrible quote from my youth. I thought it would age well, and it just didn't."

"What was it?" I ask as she fixes her dress.

"No. It was so bad." She giggles.

"Now you *have* to tell me!" I beg.

"It was a journey song," she says, grimacing. I try to hold it back, but I can't, so I burst out laughing and Tessa joins me. "I was young! At least my artist was able to cover it up."

"Yes, thank goodness." I laugh. "Are you going to look for an artist here now?"

"Eventually, yes. I don't have any current plans for tattoos, but the needle is always calling. Oh god, that did *not* sound good. I just meant I enjoy getting tattoos." She takes a sip of the wine the waiter just placed in front of us.

"My friend, Shiloh, has a ton of tattoos. I think she goes somewhere in the city. I'll ask her next time I see her, she has beautiful tattoos," I say.

"Yes, please. I have to ask Paige, too. I noticed a few of hers but haven't had the chance to ask her about them." Tessa smiles.

"I think she goes to the city, too. There really isn't anyone local who does them, unfortunately. There used to be a guy who did, but there wasn't enough traffic, so he moved to the city," I explain.

"Totally understandable. It's a specific clientele, or you need to have cheap rent to keep the place open," Tessa says.

"Mac and cheese bites." The waiter places them in the middle of the table and disappears toward the kitchen.

"Holy shit, those look delicious," Tessa says, grabbing one. She takes a bite of one and groans. It's a beautiful sound to my ears. As she chews, she moans and groans again. She's fucking killing me right now. I take a sip of my wine to distract myself. "You have to try one!"

Tessa pushes the plate toward me, and I grab one. Holy crap, they really are good. Now I'm the one moaning, but I don't care. Why can't mac and cheese bites be available everywhere?

Tessa and I talk through dinner. Between bites, she tells me about living in Boston and how she met her ex—he seems like a dick, but I keep my observations to myself. It's bad enough that he treated her like shit, but he seems to be doing the same thing to the kids—her wonderful kids, who don't deserve any of that. She's taking it in stride, trying not to project her feelings of him onto her kids. My mother did the same with my father. He wasn't around, and whenever I questioned it, she didn't tell me a lie or badmouth him; she gave me the truth. He wasn't ready to be a father and didn't stick around. It wasn't until I was older that I realized my father leaving me also meant he left my mother.

"So, I have to be honest about something," I start.

"Okay…" Tessa stiffens, her body going tense with anxiety.

"I caught Natalie sneaking out last weekend. She wasn't getting far, and I made her turn right back around. We talked for a few minutes about what was going on. She misses her friends in Boston, and she promised me she'd try to talk to you about it. I didn't want to stress you, and I didn't want to betray her trust, but I think as her mom, you should know," I explain.

"Wow." Tessa looks at me, speechless. "Thank you for telling me. She did come to me and explained how she missed her friends, and she's actually with them this weekend in Boston.

I'm so glad you caught her, but I'm also glad you gave her a chance to talk to me first."

I let out a breath of relief. "Thank God. I was worried I did the wrong thing. I just wanted to make sure she was safe."

Tessa takes my hand from across the table. "There's no right answer when it comes to being a parent. But the fact that you made sure she got home safe and talked to her when she was upset means more than I can explain."

"I have a Ring camera in the front and backyard by the way, so if she tries it again, I'll be on it," I joke.

"Hopefully she's learned her lesson. I can't say I wasn't a rebellious teenager myself, but that's a story for another time." She laughs.

I pay the check and take Tessa's hand in mine as we walk to my car. I drive back to Evergreen Valley and head for the elementary school. The parking lot is almost at capacity, but that's to be expected. I don't think I'll see Jax tonight, but supposedly Shiloh is around here somewhere. Across the room, I spot her in a bright red Santa suit as she climbs behind the stage.

"That's my best friend, Shiloh. But I didn't know she was in the play." I laugh, pointing her out to Tessa.

We take our seats, and it's adorable, but my attention is on Tessa. About half way through the play, she put her left hand on my thigh, and I haven't been able to focus since. I know it's a kids play, and she isn't trying to start anything here. But her touch is addictive and distracting as hell. All I want to do is kiss her. I've been thinking about it since our first kiss in the library, but the moment hasn't been right. I almost kissed her when we were leaving the restaurant, but then an old couple was holding the door open for us, and it would've been awkward to stop and kiss.

I think she can feel the tension I'm fighting. I'm trying to focus on anything else, but her hand is emitting a heat I can feel through my dress and tights. You'd think with double the fabric I wouldn't have to worry about that, but unfortunately, I can feel everything. Or maybe I'm imagining it. Tessa is smirking in my direction, her red-lipped smile curved up to one side. She's definitely trying to torture me. I only wish I was able to torture her back. Maybe I'll get the chance to later. Of course, the thought of that only makes her hand on my thigh more of a torture.

Toward the end, Shiloh, dressed as Santa Claus, comes on stage. Apparently one of the teachers got sick and couldn't dress up, and Shiloh was the only one willing to do it. We head out just as the play ends. We're walking out of the building when Tessa stops me. She pulls me by the arm, and I freeze. She's looking up at the ceiling, so I glance up. There's a fresh piece of mistletoe hanging above the door frame. I smile and look back at Tessa.

Without thinking about it, I pull her in for a kiss. Her lips feel like two soft pillows as they collide with mine. I completely forget how to breathe or kiss for a brief moment. I've been with women before, even older women, but this is like something I've never experienced. She swings her arm around my neck, and I pull her closer to me. We eventually pull apart, not wanting to make a scene in the elementary school.

"Wow…" I murmur, looking at her red lips. Her lipstick isn't the least bit smudged. I wonder what brand she uses? I'll have to ask her later.

"Do you wanna head home and continue this there?" Tessa asks, and I nod.

ELEVEN

Tessa

"Do you mind if we go to my place? I have to let Rumi out," I say.

"Of course." Parker nods.

We walk across her driveway and up the path to the house. I unlock the front door and let Rumi out the back. Parker takes off her shoes and waits by the front door awkwardly.

"Please, make yourself at home, you can sit anywhere," I tell her. "Do you want anything to drink?"

"No thanks," she calls before taking a seat on one of the couches.

I bring Rumi back in and dry off her paws from the snow. She finds her favorite toy and settles next to the heater in the kitchen. She looks relaxed as I grab myself a cup of water. I'm not thirsty, but it's to buy myself some time. It was my big idea to bring Parker over, and I wanted to, but now that she's here…what does this mean? I shaved my entire body, just in case. But am I ready to sleep with her? Am I ready to take that next step? I don't know. It's been almost twenty years since I'd been on a first date. Even longer since I'd slept with someone who wasn't Weston. Sure, I've slept with women before, but not for a very long time. It has to be like riding a bike, right?

"Are you okay?" Parker asks, startling me. I drop the cup straight into the sink, but thankfully, it's pure plastic and only makes a loud sound.

"Sorry, you scared me," I admit.

"Are you nervous or something? I can head home if you want to call it a night. It's not like it's a far commute," she jokes.

"No, I just…" I sigh. "I haven't exactly been on a first date in a long time. And I haven't been with a woman for even longer than that. Not that I don't know what I'm doing, but it's like getting on a bike for the first time in almost twenty years. Did they change anything? Does everyone still go in the same direction? I don't know. I'm just overthinking it."

Parker stands in front of me and grabs my left arm, squeezing my hand gently. "We can take this as slow or as fast as you want. I don't have any expectations for tonight. I just want to spend more time with you. If we're kissing, that's cool. If more happens, that's cool, too. If not, I'm just happy spending time with you. But if you're worried about anything in particular we can talk about it."

"Thank you, that makes me feel better." I smile. I can practically feel my anxiety slipping away when I look at Parker. It isn't gone entirely, and I'm sure it will be back, but knowing Parker cares about more than sex is reassuring.

I take Parker by the hand and lead her back to the living room. We sit on the couch side by side, and she brushes my hair out of my face. I blush as her fingers creep across my cheeks. She touches my cheek, then traces her fingers along my lips. I can still feel the impression of her lips from earlier.

"What lipstick do you use? I'm amazed it hasn't smudged," Parker says.

I laugh, thrown off by the question. "I'm honestly not sure. Is that what you're thinking about right now?"

"Sorry, I was admiring your lips thinking about kissing you, but then I was impressed by your lipstick." She giggles.

"Let's test out it's durability." I bite down on my bottom lip before leaning in to kiss her.

Parker relaxes as I use my free hand to touch her neck. She slides her tongue inside my mouth, and I instinctively groan. She pulls me in closer and kisses softly down my neck. She peppers delicate, soft, and slow kisses up to my ear before lightly tugging on my earlobe. If she keeps this up, we'll be in my bedroom sooner than later. Her lips meet mine again, and we can't stop kissing. We only take short breaks for air, unable to control ourselves.

"Come here." She pulls me onto her lap, and I wrap my legs around her hips, straddling her.

"Fuck, I like this," I whisper against her lips.

"Me too," she whispers back.

Our tongues tangle together, and my eyes flutter close in pleasure. Parker grips my ass, holding me as my sweater dress starts riding up my ass. I still have my tights on, but they're barely doing anything. I can feel her hands on the curve of my ass, and I gently rock my hips on her. Everything about this feels natural. I don't have to think or worry about my next move. Parker's body seems to complement mine in all the best ways. She hums against me as I lean my chest into hers.

If I had known it would feel like this, I might've said yes to her earlier. Even though…that probably isn't true. I'm glad I trusted my gut and didn't jump into a date with Parker. It helped me see that she isn't someone who takes no for an answer. Plus, she's incredibly kind and has the best heart.

"God, you're so beautiful." I push her red hair out from her face and hold her face with my hand.

She bats her dark lashes, her cheeks pinking up with desire. She has freckles across both her cheeks. I look down and can see down the top of her dress—there's pink lace peeking out. Fuck, I want to know exactly what she looks like…everywhere. Am I crazy to want to take this further? I know I can go at my pace with Parker. She's someone who makes me feel safe.

"What are you thinking?" Parker raises an eyebrow at me.

"I was wondering if you want to take this to my bedroom?" I tilt my head and look at her bashfully.

"Fuck, yes. I was hoping you'd ask." She kisses me chastely and scoops me up.

In one swift movement she's carrying me in her arms down the hallway to my bedroom. How the hell is she so strong? I wouldn't have ever expected it from her. She has such a petite frame. My bedroom is easy to tell apart from the kids' rooms. Theirs are decorated with their names, and mine is not. Parker pushes the door open with her foot and sets me down carefully on the bed.

"We don't have to do anything, but this bed has to be more comfortable than the couch." She laughs.

"How the hell did you get so strong?" I ask, looking her over. She's walking around my bedroom, looking at the art I've put up.

"I take self-defense classes. I like to know I can protect myself." She shrugs. Her red hair cascades down her slender back.

I sit on the edge of the bed and decide to get out of my tights. But of course, it's not really simple with one hand. I'm twisting my body when Parker turns around and kneels before me. If you've never had a woman kneeling before you, you're missing out. I'm immediately soaked. Parker doesn't speak, running her hand up the bottom of my thigh, and I squeal when she gets close to my pussy. She freezes, her hands not moving as she looks at me, clearly worried she did something wrong. I shake my head and she continues. She gently pulls the tights down my legs, trying not to tear them, before sliding her hands down the back of my legs. I can feel her manicured fingertips brush against my calf and then lift my ankle onto her shoulder to take the tights off completely. She tosses them to the side and looks up at me, smirking.

"Well, ain't this a beautiful view." She bites down on her pink bottom lip and lets go of my ankles.

She stands above me, tilting my face to look at her. I have goosebumps all over my skin—except for where my nipples are hard like rocks. They poke through my bra and sweater, and I know she can see them. But right now, her focus is on my eyes. She uses two fingers to hold my chin up, and I look into her light eyes and beg for her to do more. She smirks, taking the time to tease me while doing absolutely nothing.

"Are you going to kiss me or make me wait?" I mutter.

"Mmm, someone's feisty. I like that." She drops my chin but it stays in place, watching her. "I need you to tell me what you want."

"Fuck, I just want you to touch me." I whimper. It's embarrassing begging for her, but I don't care. She's eating it up, and I'm desperate.

"Why don't you show me how?" She smirks.

"I can't." I sigh.

"You can't touch yourself?" She looks at me confused.

"My arm?" I hold up the cast. I couldn't maneuver the right way to touch myself ever since they put it on. And I don't have the same strength in my left hand.

"What if I let you borrow my arm?"

"What?" Now I'm the confused one.

"Why don't you take off your panties and sit back on the bed. If you want," she adds quickly.

I kick off the red lace panties and sit on my bed. She climbs on the bed behind me and leaves one leg on either side of me. I lean back into her warmth and wait for her to tell me more. She reaches her right arm under mine.

"Tell me what to do, and I can be your arm," she whispers.

"Oh." My mouth forms a little O as I realize that's what she meant. She wants to help me masturbate.

"Only if you want to," she adds softly, kissing my shoulder.

"Yes, I do," I say. "Touch me," I command.

Her hand slips down my hips, and her body pushes closer to me as she slips two fingers against my swollen clit.

"Fuck, you're so wet, baby. Is that all for me?" she whispers in my ear. I close my eyes, letting my head fall back on her shoulder.

Parker slides her fingers down my pussy, and I moan. "I can feel you getting wetter. Does this turn you on, baby?"

"Mmm," I hum, unable to form any coherent words.

"Tell me what you like. Tell me what you'd do if I weren't here." Her warm breath hits my ear.

"C-Circles…around…my…c-clit," I manage to say. Parkers other hand has found my breasts and is currently dipping into my bra to graze my nipples.

"Circles, okay." Parker uses her right hand and does achingly slow circles around my clit. I know she's teasing me on purpose now, but I can't take it.

"F-faster please," I beg breathlessly.

"Your wish is my command." She moans as she moves her fingers faster.

"Can you ch-choke me?" I ask.

"Hell, yes," Parker murmurs.

She takes her hand from my breasts, giving each nipple one last tug, before wrapping her left hand around my throat. I moan, whimpering as her other hand moves in circles. I'm dripping all over her hand, and I don't have it in me to care. We can clean her up later. For now, all I want is the orgasm I'm desperately chasing.

"Fuck, you're *soaked*. And you're all *mine*," Parker says.

I clench my fist in the sheets, holding on tightly as I feel my release rising. It feels good—being called hers. It feels right. Like I was always meant to be. I relax just for a second, and then I'm screaming Parker's name.

"Yes! Parker! Yes! Yes!" I shout as I see stars, and Parker doesn't let up. Her grip stays steady on my neck, and her fingers don't let up until I'm pushing them away. I collapse back into her body, and I can barely open my eyes to say thank you.

TWELVE

Parker

I brush Tessa's dark curls out of her face and reach for a tissue on the nightstand. My hand is covered in Tessa, so I quickly clean it off and toss the tissue aside. I can smell her shampoo, some kind of apple cinnamon mix. It's intoxicating. She relaxes her body against mine. I shift against her. I'm wet as hell, but this isn't the time. Tessa needs a moment to come down from her orgasm before we tackle anything else.

"I'm sorry. I can move." She goes to move off me, but I stop her, holding her body close to mine instead.

"Stay where you feel safe," I tell her, and she doesn't move—except to adjust her dress. It had creeped all the way up over her ass, giving me a nice view of her ass tat.

"It never feels this way when I do it," she mutters quietly.

I laugh. "Yeah, it's usually better when someone else does it."

Tessa climbs off my lap and sits up next to me. She's only wearing her dress, her bottom half completely bare. I reach over and help her take the dress off completely. I want to see every inch of her. There's nothing I want to miss. As I toss aside the dress, I admire her. Her body is lean and covered in tattoos. Most of them are book related or flowers, but all of them were done with such grace that they made you stop and stare. Her breasts are big, falling lower than mine, probably due to having two children. I want her to touch me, truthfully, I'm dying for it. But maybe she's a pillow princess and that isn't going to happen. It wouldn't be the first time, and it won't be a dealbreaker for me.

"Lie down," Tessa commands, as if reading my mind.

I kick off my pants and lie down as she climbs between my legs and bends down to kiss me. Her lips are soft against mine, and she tugs lightly on my bottom lip with her teeth. I moan, wiggling my hips, trying to get some sort of friction. She kisses me, stopping to lick my neck to my collar bone and then we go back to kissing.

"Mmm," she hums.

"You're killing me here," I groan.

Tessa dips her fingers to touch my pussy through my panties, and I can feel myself getting wetter. Somehow it's equally evil and hot. Why can't she just fuck me already? She moves her hand off my pussy and uses it to steady herself as she kisses me. It must be a pain in the ass to have only one good hand and arm right now. I'm taking full advantage of having both and touching every inch of her skin. I don't know how she tastes yet, but I can smell her arousal. Her pussy presses against my bare thigh, and I moan, feeling her wetness against my skin. She grinds down lightly, maintaining eye contact with me as she does so.

"Come on," I whimper. I'm not above begging. I need this.

Tessa laughs before sliding her body down my chest and pressing her face to my pussy. She moves my panties to the side and licks my clit.

"Oh fuck!" I scream the moment her tongue touches me.

She sucks on my clit, only making me wetter. I'm whimpering, pulling on her hair tightly with my fingers. I'm touching my breasts, tugging on my nipples and teasing myself. At the same time, she flattens her tongue, swiping it across my clit. I cry out for her. She says something, but it's all muffled between her thighs. My grip on her hair gets tighter as she licks me.

My hips buck as she sticks her tongue inside me. She then licks up and down my pussy and dips in two fingers, swirling them around inside me, folding them to hit my G-spot. I'm so fucking close, and I want to come so bad. Never have I ever been so close to finishing with someone before. But Tessa seems to know exactly how to touch me and where all my triggers are. She hums on my clit, sucking it while pumping her fingers in and out of me. My head falls back as far as it can go, and my back raises off the bed.

"Fuck yes! Tess! Yes!" I call out.

I collapse into the pillows and need a moment to catch my breath. I've had a lot of good sex in my life, but holy shit. This is something else entirely. Tessa smiles as she wipes her mouth and sucks her fingers dry. I shiver, watching her clean the last of me off her hand. She lies down next to me, quietly waiting for me to say something.

"Wow," I say, and Tessa smiles.

"I'm a bit rusty, but I'm glad to know I still got it." She giggles.

"Has it been that long since you've been with a woman?" I ask raising an eyebrow. It doesn't seem likely, but I'm curious.

"Yes, I dated a few women in college before I was with Weston. I was married for almost twenty years, so it's a bit different for me. I didn't think being with a woman again was in the cards for me," she explains. "Have you ever been with men?"

"I have. I'm the kind of bi where men aren't my first choice, but they seem to be easier to find," I joke.

"Oh, yes. Women, especially good women, are snatched up right away and then in committed relationships for years," Tessa jokes.

"I usually try to go for vibes. It's been mostly women lately, but that's because I've been spending a lot of time in bars. There aren't too many other places to meet people in a small town," I admit.

"That makes sense. I wouldn't even know where to start if you hadn't knocked on my door." She blushes.

"Oh, yeah? Is that all I had to do?"

"I'm serious. This was the last thing I was looking for." She pauses. "But I'm glad it happened."

I reach for her hand, intertwining my fingers with hers. I brush over her painted red nails—that thankfully aren't too long. Rubbing my thumb across the back of her hand, I say, "I am too."

In the morning, I wake up before Tessa. I hear her alarm—that she must have on automatically—and after checking that it isn't actually a phone call or an emergency, I shut it off. Tessa is sleeping soundly, her mouth wide open and her hair a mess all over her pillow. She looks so beautiful; I almost climb back into bed with her. But instead, I head to her kitchen and look for something to eat. I want to make her pancakes or something in bed, but all I can find is cereal and milk. I set up the bowls on the counter and decide that coffee might be a better way to start the day. I make it black and carry all her sugar, creamer, and milk to the bedroom.

"Good morning," I say quietly and place the stuff on the nightstand.

I sit on the side of the bed and kiss her cheek, pushing her dark curls out of her eyes as she opens them and looks at me. Smiling, she sits up and stretches, her breasts falling free from the sheets. My cheeks heat up, and I bite down on my bottom lip.

"Good morning." She leans in to kiss me.

"I made coffee." I pick up the mug and hand it to her. "But I wasn't sure how you take it."

"Three sugars and a little creamer." She smiles. I help her add what she needs, and she takes a sip, letting out a satisfied sound.

"Your alarm went off, but I silenced it. I figured you're allowed to sleep in," I explain.

"Yeah, I don't start working on the weekends until the new year." She nods.

"Every weekend?" I frown.

"Nope. I'll have a more flexible schedule come then. I'm still working out all the details with my boss," she explains. "Mmm, this is so good. You don't want any?"

"I was thinking about having something else for breakfast." I wiggle my brow and look at her suggestively.

"Oh." She blushes and puts the mug down. "Yes, please."

I pull her in for a kiss, and if either of us has morning breath I can't tell. All I can feel are her lips on mine and our bodies fusing together. We're only separated by a thin sheet, and she throws it off of herself as I climb on top of her. Straddling her body, I put my hand around her neck, just the way she likes. Tessa's head falls backward, and I rub my finger across her bottom lip.

"Don't be a tease," she mutters.

So I pull her into me, our tongues tangling and teeth colliding from the roughness. I want to fuck her, and I want to hear her beg for it. I grab her breasts, each one overflowing in my small hands. Her nipples are hard as rocks as I lick my way down her stomach. I stop above her pubic bone, giving her little nibbles. I drag one hand back up to her neck and squeeze lightly.

"Oh!" she moans, her body reacting to my touch.

I lift her leg over mine and twist my body so our pussies are hovering over the other. Her breathing deepens as mine becomes heavy. It's not the easiest position, especially when one of us doesn't have a working arm. But I'm determined. I hold her thigh on top of my own and grind my clit against her, causing her to scream.

"P-P-Parker! Oh my god!" she cries out in pleasure.

"Don't worry, baby. I'll do the work." I wink and use my free arm to keep it gripped around her throat. Not too tight and just enough pressure.

Tessa hums. Her moans escape her lips as I rock my hips back and forth. I can feel her pussy leaking into mine as we move. She bucks her hips, desperate for me to move more and get more friction. I'm going for a slow and steady pace, but if she needs more, I'll gladly give her that. I want to give her whatever she needs. She looks like a fucking sex goddess moaning under me. Her makeup is smudged, and her hair is knotty. Her perfect fucking tits are bouncing around as my pussy drips against hers.

"Fuck, you're so sexy," I say with a groan.

Moving my hand from her throat, I drag it toward her mouth. I push two fingers between her lips so she can suck on them, and then I drag them down the center of her chest. I twirl my wet fingers across her breasts as I rock my hips back and forth. I want her to scream my name by the time I make her come. I lean down to bite gently on each of her pebbled nipples, and she whimpers. Like something out of a freaking porno, she makes sounds I didn't know were possible—sounds I always thought were fake until I hear them coming from her lips.

"I'm so fucking c-close," she says, her eyes clamped shut as I move my hips faster.

"Look at me. I want you to see who makes you feel this good," I tell her. I don't even know where this is coming from, but I like it. I'm not usually so controlling in bed. Tessa seems to bring out a new side of me.

Her eyes shoot open, then close again. It's like they're glued shut but she's trying with all her strength to break free. I flick my wrist over my pussy and then hers, watching as she comes undone beneath me.

Exploding like fireworks, my own personal show.

THIRTEEN

Tessa

___

The kids come back late Sunday night, long after I've sent Parker home. We might've broken the record for how many orgasms we gave each other. The second she left, I threw the sheets in the washing machine. I left the pillow cases on, still smelling of Parker's perfume, but there's too much evidence of our weekend together. Even Rumi is looking at me knowingly. I end up giving her extra treats to keep her quiet. Not that I think she'd somehow tell the kids, but I feel like a teenager who is covering their bases to avoid getting caught.

The kids are so exhausted, and they rattle off updates about the weekend on their way to bed. Even Natalie is smiling. She hugs me before bed, too, which doesn't happen often.

I'm calling it a night too, exhausted from all the sex I had with Parker. Who knew sex could take that much out of you? I guess when you're going at it for hours at a time, it's to be expected. I make myself a quick bedtime snack and FaceTime Parker.

I'm balancing my phone in one hand with the bowl of strawberries I just cut up. I make it to my bedroom and close the door behind me. I prop the phone on the nightstand, and that's when

I notice the rolls of wrapping paper hanging out of my closet door. Holy fucking shit. What day is today?! I race to the calendar and look at the days. How the hell is it the night before Christmas Eve already? Didn't we just move in?

"Babe? You okay? You look like you're panicking," Parker says seriously.

"I totally forgot to wrap the kids presents," I whisper.

"Like…all of them?" Parker's eyes go wide.

"Yes! I didn't have time and then my arm…Oh my God! How am I going to do it with one arm!?" I take a deep breath as I see Parker getting out of bed. "Where are you going?" I ask, picking up the phone.

"Obviously I'm coming over to help." She's putting on a pair of sweatpants.

"You don't—"

"Don't even bother. Give me like five minutes, and I'll be over." She hangs up before I can protest, and I sign. So much for that early night.

Five minutes later, she texts that she's outside, and I let her in. Her coat and hat are covered in fresh snow, and she's shaking when she comes in. She lines up her boots by the door and kisses me chastely after checking her surroundings first. She follows me to the bedroom, and I show her the closet full of toys for Drew and clothes and things for Natalie.

"Damn, okay. No wonder you need my help. Did you rob a mall?" She laughs.

"It was probably divorce guilt, but I wanted to go a little bigger than normal." I shrug.

"Okay, why don't you give me the stuff, and I'll be on wrapping duty?" she suggests.

"You seriously don't have to do this—"

"I know, but I *want* to. So let me." She takes my hand, and I nod.

I grab things one at a time and bring them to Parker where she's sitting on the floor with the tape, scissors, and wrapping paper. To make it easier, I keep Drew and Natalie's stuff in different piles. Apparently Parker is some kind of wrapping savant, because she's able to wrap them beautifully and faster than I ever anticipated.

"I used to watch YouTube videos on how to wrap gifts because it was something I was bad at," Parker explains.

"I'm terrible, but that's just what people get," I joke.

"My mom was always good at it; it was so annoying. I never knew how she did it."

"My mom had someone else do it. Every year, she'd let the stores she shopped at wrap them for her. She hated it, and my dad never wanted to. He said it was a girl's job," I say, rolling my eyes.

"Oh, God." Parker makes a face.

"In his defense, he's since come around. But yeah, I'm with you." I shrug.

"Did you have any Christmas traditions growing up?" she asks, looking up at me. I sit on the edge of the bed, taking a break from moving the presents.

"We baked cookies from scratch for Santa every year, even after we stopped believing. My dad would sneak downstairs and eat the cookies just as he always did. And my cousins and I would always get to open one gift on Christmas Eve. It had to be the smallest one, but it was still exciting," I explain with a smile.

"I love that. My mom collected snow globes so we always went on a hunt during the holidays to add to her collection. And we picked our own tree every year from a local tree farm." Parker smiles.

"Wow, did you cut it down and everything?"

"Sometimes. I wasn't the biggest fan, but my mom enjoyed it, so I tried. Eventually I convinced her to let us grab one of the precut trees." Parker laughs.

"Next year I want to take the kids to get a real tree. We didn't have the time this year." I sigh.

"Do you have any traditions you do with them?" Parker asks.

"Yes, actually. We decorate gingerbread houses together every year. It's my favorite thing to do with them. We bake them from scratch, too."

"Wow, that's impressive," Parker says in awe.

I stand up, grabbing the last of the presents from the closet and moving the wrapped ones back into the closet. I'd label each one before I put it in, but since Drew still believes, I need to hide these until *Santa* delivers them. Natalie plays along for her brother but she stopped believing already.

"Thank you so much for your help. I wouldn't have been able to do this without you," I admit.

"I truly don't mind."

I take a seat next to Parker on the floor and watch as she wraps. I yawn, exhausted from the long day. At least I don't have work tomorrow. I lean my head against the foot of the bed and watch as she works. She's got it down to a science, knowing exactly how much wrapping paper she needs for each present. My eyes flutter shut, and the next thing I know, Parker is shaking me awake.

"What? Oh, shit." I look around at the stack of wrapped presents. "I'm so sorry! I didn't mean to doze off. How long was I out?"

"Maybe an hour? But it's fine. You're cute when you drool," Parker teases. I rub the corners of my mouth—totally dry.

"I was going to let you sleep, but I heard Drew looking for you," Parker says. And on cue, Drew knocks on my door. I look at Parker anxiously, but she jumps up and hides on the other side of the bed on the floor.

"Drew? What are you doing up, honey?" I open the door halfway and look at my sleepy eyed kid. He's dressed in his Minecraft pajamas and has sleep lines on his forehead.

"I needed an extra hug. I had a bad dream." He frowns.

"Of course. Let me walk you back to bed." I lead him back down the hall after making sure he doesn't have to use the bathroom.

"Can you tuck me extra good?" he asks with a smile.

"Of course I can." I kiss his forehead and grab his four blankets. It used to be one, but then he begged for another, and now I'm constantly having to fight with him when he brings up needing more.

"I love you. Sleep tight." I kiss both his cheeks and make sure his nightlight is on.

"Love you, mama." He closes his eyes and drifts right back to sleep.

I take the time to peek in on Natalie. I have no idea what time it is, so I'm not surprised when I find her up and watching something on her iPad. She smiles at me, and I close the door, deciding to let her stay up. I know there are worse things she could be doing.

"Are they okay?" Parker asks as I get back to my bedroom.

The floor is all cleaned up, the stack of presents in my closet, and the supplies on my dresser. Parker's sitting on my bed, and I close the door behind me.

"Yeah, he has bad dreams sometimes, so I just tucked him in again," I explain.

"I'm all done with the presents…unless you have more?" she asks, almost hopefully, probably thinking I'm going to ask her to leave.

"Do you think you can stay for a bit?" I ask.

"Of course, what do you need?" She looks around for another task, but instead, I take her hand.

"I just want to spend some time with you. No need to do anything," I say.

"Oh, then yes. I thought maybe you'd be too tired."

"I'm wide awake now that I got my nap," I joke.

Parker and I lie down in my bed, facing each other. Her red hair is pulled back into a tight bun with just a few loose ends falling out. She's not wearing any makeup, probably from the shower she took when she got home. I can see all her freckles perfectly. Parker turns her neck and winces.

"Are you okay?"

"Yeah, just a little sore. I'm okay though." She holds the side of her neck and pushes on it lightly.

"Is it because of the wrapping?" I ask.

She makes a face like she's trying not to say yes but also trying not to lie.

"Flip onto your stomach," I say.

"What? Why?" She raises an eyebrow.

"Just trust me!"

Parker gets up and flips onto her stomach, her legs at the end of the bed, her head face down on the pillow. I climb over her carefully, straddling her ass. She looks up at me with heat in her gaze, probably thinking something completely off. I use my good hand to rub her neck. Taking turns on each side, I massage and add pressure. Parker moans and I giggle.

"You can't make sounds like that if you want me to stay focused," I warn her.

"Mmm." She nods.

I use my casted elbow on her back to add pressure and match my other one. The cast is bulky and annoying, but at least I'm not in any sort of pain. Most of the time, I just ignore it if I can. I'm learning to do more things than I expected with my left hand. I focus on Parker's neck, since that's what's bothering her, but the more I add pressure, the more sounds she makes. She's moaning softly and humming in pleasure, causing me to feel the heat between my thighs. I can't even clench them together without squishing them against her ass.

Am I really so horny that I can't even give Parker a massage without thinking about her naked? It isn't my fault that she has a perfect body. We slept together less than twelve hours ago, and I came an ungodly amount of times...but holy shit. Just thinking about her and feeling her underneath me makes me want to touch her again.

"If you want to fuck me, you can just ask," Parker says with a giggle.

"I'm giving you a massage!" I exclaim.

"Mmm, and you could be giving me an orgasm instead. I'm pretty sure either way, my neck pain will be gone," Parker says, lifting her head to look back at me.

"God, you're so bad." I shake my head.

My hands drift to her sides and then wrap around as I reach for her breasts. If I'm going to do this, I'm at least going to tease her first.

FOURTEEN

Parker

Tessa's on my back, giving me one of the best massages of my life, but I can tell she wants more. She's grinding her hips against my, ass and every time I make a sound, her breath hitches like she can't control herself. It's so cute to see her turned on and desperately trying not to be. It's nice that she's taking the time to do something for me. I didn't mind wrapping all the presents, but it did end up hurting my neck—which sucks. Tessa is observant, often noticing the small things that I haven't yet said out loud. If I don't ask her for things when I need them, I'll be a hypocrite, but I also don't want to add anything to her plate. So it's nice that she's able to see what I need.

Tessa touches the sides of my breasts and moves her hand down my side. I can tell she's trying to tease me. She goes back to massaging my back and neck, using her good hand to squeeze on the side that hurts. Then she bends down, leaning so her breasts are pressed against my back, and she grinds her hips on my ass. I let out a quiet moan, trying not to scar her children for life. Tessa knows she can just fuck me, but she's taking her time with it. So I let her touch my breasts, well, just one since she can only reach one right now. Then she climbs off my body and flips me over and smirks at me before leaning in to kiss my neck.

"I'm going to show you how thankful I am for all you do," she whispers in a sultry tone in my ear before biting the side of my neck. I let out a louder moan, and Tessa's hand immediately covers my mouth. I grin beneath her palm. It's secretly a bit hot.

She bites the side of my neck, sucking a little harder this time, and I try to stay quiet, but she's slowly stoking the fire. I hum against her hand as she moves down my neck, sucking gently. I wonder if she's trying to leave a mark on purpose. I haven't had a hickey since high school, but here I am letting this milf of a woman brand me. It's sexy, knowing she wants me as much as I want her. We haven't really talked about it. Our first date turned into a lesbian stereotype of a non-ending sexual adventure.

Tessa moves her hand off my mouth so she can kiss me. Her pouty lips crush mine with passion. She pulls me toward her, letting her thigh slip between my legs. I moan into her mouth as I grind my pussy against her. She kisses me, grabbing my ass with her good hand as she lets me grind against her thigh. Whenever I kiss her, she makes me forget how to breathe. It's like we share the same breath, and neither of us want to stop. My nipples are hard, popping against the thin fabric of my sweater. I hadn't thought to put on a bra, knowing the kids were already asleep, and I'd be alone with Tessa. They rub against the soft fabric, touching Tessa's breasts through her thin sleep shirt, and we both groan.

"I want to go down on you, but you have to be quiet., she whispers and looks at me seriously. It's the same look a teacher gives their student to show them they mean business. I swallow hard and nod.

Tessa gets up, opens her bedroom door, and listens for a moment before closing it and locking it behind her. She strips down to just her panties—no bra—and I take a moment to admire her. She's so fucking gorgeous. She's standing before me in black cotton panties, and I can't wait for her to touch me again. How the hell did I get this lucky? She climbs back into the bed, and I rest on her pillows, propping myself up a bit so I can watch her.

"Can I?" Tessa asks, tugging on my sweatpants.

"Yes." I nod. She pulls them down with one hand, and I help her kick them off.

My thong is soaked, and barely does anything to conceal how fucking turned on I am. Tessa takes a second to admire it before pressing her tongue against my pussy. I gasp, unable to quiet myself, and she looks up at me with a warning in her eyes. I nod and she taps my thighs, telling me to lift my ass. She takes off the thong with her teeth. I groan as she slides it down my thighs. God, I'm in heaven with this woman.

"Mmm, you're so wet for me," she murmurs against my skin. She kisses the insides of my thighs, nibbling lightly, and I grab the sheets to keep me from moaning.

"You're killing me," I say with a groan.

"No, I'm *thanking* you," she says with a smirk.

Before I have a chance to reply, she bends down to lick my pussy. The second her tongue touches my clit, I'm a goner. I see her ass in the air, the fire flame tattoo on the side of her cheek. She slides her tongue through my slit, and I see stars. My knuckles have to be white from how hard I'm gripping the sheets. Tessa is holding my body against the bed with her hand just above my pubic bone as she licks. I can feel her tongue swirling and twisting around my pussy as she tries to get every last drip of me. I want to moan, but I also don't want this to end.

"Mmm, you taste so good," she hums against me, taking a second to breathe as she kisses my thighs again with her soaked lips.

"*Tess...*" I moan.

She goes back to licking my pussy, this time harder as she sucks on my clit. My thighs clamp around her head, and I reach to grab her hair. I grip the dark ponytail that's messily falling out of the hair tie, and she fucking whimpers against me. I pull harder, and she does it again, only fueling my orgasm.

"Yes, yes. Don't stop," I say as quietly as I can manage.

Tessa doesn't stop as she sucks on my clit, and I come hard and quiet. I'm biting down on the side of my own hand to keep from crying out her name. I can't control my breathing, but hopefully it isn't as loud as it sounds in my head. I let go of Tessa's hair and collapse on the bed, my thighs freeing her head and my eyes fluttering open. Holy fucking shit, the mouth on Tessa is lethal.

She smiles, wiping her mouth off on the sheets and climbing closer to me. She leans in to kiss me softly once on the lips and then lies down next to me. She smiles, her cherry-red lips shiny from the remnants of what she's done to me.

"How was that for a thank you?" she asks.

"I think I should do things for you more often. Have any dishes that need washing or something?" I joke.

"You do more than enough. I wish I could do more than give you orgasms." She sighs, looking away.

I grab her face and force her to look at me. "You don't have to give me anything. I don't want this to be a relationship where you keep track or think you owe me things. I like being with you, and being in your life is enough for me," I admit.

"Relationship?" Her eyes widen, and her cheeks redden to match her lips.

"I mean, we did sort of turn our first date into a weekend adventure." I laugh.

"I thought that was just a lesbian thing." She lets out a chuckle along with me.

"If you're not ready to call it a relationship, I can wait. But just know there's no one else in the meantime. I'm ready to get to know you and do whatever I can to make this real," I say honestly. It's scary, but I have more to lose if I'm not honest. I don't want to play it cool. I want to show her how I really feel.

"I like the idea of a relationship, as long as we can still take it slow with the kids," she says.

"Of course. I'm your friend and neighbor—until you're ready to tell them more. I wouldn't expect it any other way." I smile.

Tessa leans in to kiss me, and I'm reminded of how naked she is and how horny she must be. I slide my hand down the front of her chest, stopping to tug at both of her nipples and down the front of her panties. She gasps, her mouth forming a cute little O as I press the palm of my hand against her core.

"Tess, can I please get my Christmas present early and have you sit on my face?" I ask with a wicked smirk. She shivers, her whole body shaking lightly as she nods.

"Oh my god. Yes, please." She smiles.

I get up, adjusting the pillows and lying down so she has room to grip the headboard. I help her take off her panties and throw them on the floor. Then I help her up, not wanting her to lose her balance due to her arm. She hovers over my face, and I look at her dripping pussy. Her lips glisten with her sweetness, just begging to be licked.

"I don't know if my knees are what they used to be." She laughs nervously.

"Get comfortable baby, I'm enjoying the view," I say.

She looks down at me and giggles, then bends her knees and grips the headboard with one hand. Finally, she sits on my face, her clit touching my nose and my tongue licking her folds. She tastes so Goddamn sweet. Like she's a candy invented just for me. I flatten my tongue, feeling all of her pussy on me as she rocks her hips slowly against my face. I lick from her clit all the way back and forth—she's panting, trying not to be too loud. So I suck harder on her clit, showing her how difficult it is to be quiet. She's gripping the headboard tightly and looking down at me angrily. Who would've known it's possible to look both aroused and angry at the same time.

"Oh my God, Parker," she murmurs. Her thighs close around

my head, and I suck on her clit, using my hand to slide a finger inside her pussy. She gasps and I wait as she tightens around it.

"Mmm," I hum against her.

"*Parker…*" She groans and I smile.

Pleasing a woman might just be my favorite thing to do, but pleasing Tessa? I can't imagine pleasuring anyone else could ever feel like this. If we don't work out, I'll spend the rest of my Goddamn life trying to find someone who feels and tastes this fucking good. I'm addicted, and I'm not even trying to hide it.

"Parker! Don't stop!" Her scream was a little loud that time, but I don't think she noticed. She's too focused on finishing, and I'm not going to be the one to deny her that.

She rocks her hips faster against my face, her thighs locked around my ears like she's trying to stay on one of those mechanical bulls. I suck on her clit, my finger pushing in and out of her as she comes on my face. She collapses, literally falling into the bed next to me, and I jump up to make sure she's okay. She looks so blissed out, like she's experienced something euphoric…

And it's true. We have.

FIFTEEN

Tessa

"Mom? Why is your door locked?" Drew calls through my bedroom door.

I open one of my eyes and yawn. I don't remember falling asleep last night, but I guess I must have after Parker wrapped the presents for me. Wait, then we had sex, but I don't remember her leaving. My eyes shoot open, and I realize Parker's next to me fast asleep. Fuck. I don't remember anything after we had sex, but then again, that orgasm was so good I could barely remember my name.

"Parker!" I whisper-yell and shake her. She stirs awake and opens her eyes wide.

"What?" she says groggily.

"My kids are up!" I whisper-yell.

"Mom!" Drew calls again.

"One minute, honey!" I call back. Then I look down and realize I'm still naked. "I'm just getting dressed!" I lie.

"Okay." He sighs.

Parker looks at me anxiously, "How am I supposed to get out of here?"

"I don't know. I didn't think we'd fall asleep!" I curse in my head.

"I'm sorry. I didn't mean to either. I guess I closed my eyes and never opened them," Parker says as she quickly tries getting dressed.

"Mom!" Drew calls again, so I look at the clock. It's just after eleven.

"Why don't you go wake up Natalie?" I suggest. Normally we let Natalie sleep in, but it's late enough, and I need to buy a minute or two.

"Okay!" I listen for him to walk away and then look at Parker—whose waiting for me to give her a next step.

"Can you sneak out my window?" I suggest.

"That would work, but my coat and shoes are by the front door," Parker says.

"Shit!" I quickly throw on some pajamas so I'm at least dressed.

"What if we sneak you down the hall and you can leave out the front door?" I suggest.

"What about the kids?" She looks at me with wide eyes of terror, which pretty much sums up how I'm feeling.

"I'll distract them and then tell you to go. Wait here quietly with the door cracked," I tell Parker, and she nods.

I open my door, peeking out carefully, and when I don't see anyone, I close it almost all the way behind me. She stays at the open crack, just out of sight, while I race down the hallway. I stop at Natalie's room where Drew is sitting on the bed with her.

"Good morning." I smile.

"Good morning." Drew races over and hugs my legs. I bend down to his level to hug him and place a kiss on his head.

"Can you guys go let out Rumi, and I'll get breakfast started? I slept in and I just have to get ready." It isn't a total lie, and it'll buy me a few minutes.

"Okay!" Drew says cheerfully as Natalie mutters and sits up in bed. She puts on her fluffy pink slippers and follows Drew out to the kitchen where Rumi is.

I quickly race back to the bedroom and whisper to Parker, "Come on!"

Parker creeps out behind me, following me as she and I sneak out down the hall. Thankfully, you can't see the kitchen from the front door, so Parker grabs her coat and puts her boots on. I think we're in the clear as I open the door and Parker steps out... until I hear Natalie and Drew behind me.

"Parker?" Drew says in his curious voice.

"What are you doing here?" Natalie asks.

"Oh, um..." I can't think of a lie quick enough that's plausible for Parker to be here.

"I was coming to ask your mom if you were still coming to the auction at the library today. My friend Jax is running it and needs a final tally. I was just curious if you need a ride," Parker says quickly.

"Yes, we'll be there. We're all excited." I smile, hoping the kids bought it.

"Awesome! I'll be sure to tell Jax." Parker smiles.

"Couldn't you just have texted?" Natalie crosses her arms and raises an eyebrow.

"I forgot to charge my phone last night, so it must be dead," I add quickly.

"Yeah, I called but she didn't answer. So I thought I'd just come over since I live so close by," Parker adds.

We both know Natalie doesn't totally believe us, but she's also thirteen, so she's not going to question us any further. She shrugs and Parker says goodbye, heading to her house. I close the door and head toward the kitchen, hoping to distract everyone with breakfast.

The kids don't push the Parker thing further, and we have an uneventful morning together until it's time to get ready for the auction. We don't have to go, and I know I'm not able to donate, but it means a lot to Parker. Her best friend is at risk of losing everything, and I want to help in any way I can. We helped decorate the rec room at the library, and the place looks awesome. I hope Jax will be able to earn enough to pay off the debts she needs to.

Parker drives us over, and we're one of the first to arrive. Parker needs to help set up, and since she's driving us, we'll help, too. At least there will be a chance for the kids to meet some of the local kids they'll be in school with come next week.

"Hey, I didn't expect to see you here," Paige says to me and the kids.

"Parker gave us a ride, and we thought we could help out." I smile.

"There are kids hanging out and having a snowball fight outside if you're interested," Paige says to Natalie and Drew.

"Can we?!" Drew says excitedly as he looks at me.

I glance at Natalie, who looks equally as excited but she's trying to hide it. "Can you take your brother?"

"Sure." She nods. I can tell she's looking forward to it too.

"Now you *have* to tell me what's going on with you and Parker! I have been *dying* for the details!" Paige squeals quietly.

"We spent most of the weekend together," I whisper.

"What!?" Paige exclaims a bit too loudly, and I shush her as everyone in the room turns to look at us. "Sorry!" she apologizes and turns to me.

"We're dating, but we're taking things slow. So if the kids are around, we're just friends," I explain.

"Wow, I love that. I'm honestly so happy for you." Paige gushes.

"Are you guys here to work or just gossip about me?" Parker teases, coming up behind Paige.

"Excuse me?" Paige feigns a gasp—like she's offended.

"Come on, P. I've known you practically since birth. You're a gossip and a terrible liar." Parker laughs. "Did the kids ask anything after I left this morning?" Parker asks quietly, looking at me.

"Nope, I think we're in the clear." I smile.

"What happened this morning?" Paige asks with a raised eyebrow.

"I might have got caught sneaking out of the house." Parker shrugs with a laugh.

"Come on, man! You know you gotta go out the window if the parents are coming home," Paige teases.

I'm happy about how easily I fit in with Parker and her friends. Jax is running around, trying to make everything perfect, until Paige and Parker send her home to get changed and take a nap. She looks exhausted, so I don't blame them.

She comes back a few hours later, changed but not looking too rested. Parker said something was going on with Jax's sort-of girlfriend, but she didn't have all the details. The holidays are stressful enough, especially with a pending eviction, so I don't try to get involved.

When the auction starts, there's food, dancing, and lots of bidding. Parker is bidding on almost all of them, and it makes me wonder exactly how well-off she is. She's a homeowner at a young age and never seems to be concerned about money. I know there's money in tech, but I don't know how much. It makes me feel relieved that I won't be supporting a third person on my library program director salary. She's responsible—and that's something I value more than she knows.

The kids only come in for hot cocoa and snacks when it gets too dark to be outside. I'm happy to see Natalie smiling with a group of girls who seem about her age. Maybe she's making new friends already. Drew is dancing with a group of kids his age and has a big smile on his face. I'm relieved that I made the right choice by moving us here. It isn't just my happiness I want. It's reassuring to see my kids so happy and making friends. I was worried at first. I didn't think it would be easy to switch schools as well as towns, but they both seem to be handling it really well for the most part.

"What do you say you come over for Christmas dinner tonight?" I ask Parker toward the end of the auction.

"Like after this?" she asks.

"Yes? Is that okay? I don't think we're ready for Christmas morning, but I'd love for the kids to get to know you as my friend." I smile back.

"I'd love that. Do you need me to bring anything?" she offers.

"Nope!" I pause. "Well, how good are you at Monopoly?"

"Monopoly? I've never lost," she says proudly.

"Good. You'll be on my team then." I laugh. "We always play a round on Christmas Eve after dinner."

"Oh, you're so on. I'm there." Parker smiles and I look around the room, making sure the kids aren't paying us any attention before I reach for her hand and give it a light squeeze. It's not much, but I see the way her cheeks color, and it's enough to tell me that she feels the same way I do.

"Are you ready? It's time to count everything up," Paige says, holding the basket full of clipboards from each of the auction items.

"Yep, sure am." Parker nods.

"Good luck." I smile.

Grabbing a glass of water, I wait with everyone else as Paige and Parker count up the totals. Then we'll know if Jax made enough money to keep the bookstore afloat. I'm hoping she did. I've only been in once, back when we first moved here, but it's cute as heck. It's definitely somewhere I can see myself spending an entire day buying books. It's no surprise that I love reading, and once I get things under control again, it'll go back to being part of my nightly self-care routine.

Almost a half an hour later, Parker and Paige come out and hand Jax the envelope. Both of their faces are stoic as they walk away, and I can't even tell what Parker's thinking. Jax opens the envelope, but then Drew comes running over.

"Mom! I need to pee!" he says a little too loudly.

"Okay, honey. I'll take you." I put down my water and bring him inside the library. It's the only bathroom I know about, and I don't want to ask anyone else right now.

Drew runs in the single bathroom, and I hang outside the door. I hear him pee and flush, but I don't hear the sink run, so I send him back in to wash his hands.

"How do you always know?" he grumbles.

"It's my special mommy power," I tease. "Are you having fun?"

"Yes! I met so many people. They all go to my new school. They said they're excited to see me at school next week," he says proudly.

"Aw, that's so sweet." I smile.

We head back to the party, and everyone is in a good mood. I look around the room for Parker, but she's busy hugging Jax. I imagine that must be good news, and no one looks bummed. She spots me and races over. I think she's going to hug me, but she stops herself at the last second.

"They did it! They didn't raise enough money, but they're turning the bookstore into a landmark, which means they have more time to keep it!" Parker explains.

"Yay! I'm so glad!" I smile. All I want to do is kiss her in front of everyone—but I hold myself back.

Epilogue I

PARKER

After Jax assures me I can head home, I grab Tessa and the kids. I needed to change into something more comfortable before I had dinner with them. I was nervous, it felt like I was getting invited to an initiation or something. I knew how much it mattered that the kids liked me, and how much it would determine when Tessa told them about us. I tried to convince myself I was fine, I'd been with them tons of times over the last few weeks. But tonight felt different. I knew it was important to both of us.

"I'll head over in like a half an hour?" I ask Tessa.

"Sounds perfect, I'm making ham and Mac n cheese so I just have to put everything in the oven." She smiles.

"Parker's coming for dinner?" Natalie asks.

"Yes." Tessa smiles at the same time I ask, "Is that cool?"

"Yeah," Natalie shrugs. Which I've come to learn is teenager for 'yes'.

Tessa smiles at me and I race into my house to find something to wear. When I got home this morning and actually looked in the mirror I realized Tessa had left me several hickies on my neck. Thankfully my dress for the party was a turtleneck or there would've been no hiding them. I toss my dress aside and look for something else in my closet that could hide them. I could attempt to do makeup, but with my luck I'd spill water on my neck and expose them. I scrounge through my clothes and find a red turtleneck sweater that was comfortable so I pair it with my candy cane skirt and call it a day. I grab the gifts I wrapped early this morning and head back to Tessa's house.

I knock on the door and Natalie answers the door. "I like your skirt." She says it like it's a some sort of a test I passed.

"Thank you." I tread lightly.

Taking off my shoes and coat, I walk in further and smell the food Tessa's cooking. It all smells delicious and I was starving. I had forgotten to eat for most of the day except for a few cookies and a granola bar. I put down the bag of gifts on the coffee table in the living room and follow the scent of food into the kitchen. Rumi spots me and runs over, sniffing my leg, and jumping up so I can pet her.

"Hi Rumi," I sit on the floor and she climbs on my lap, licking my cheek.

"That means she likes you, she loves giving kisses." Drew says popping out of the kitchen.

"Well, I like her too. She's so cute." I pet her, ruffling her fur as she keeps licking my face.

"Oh! Parker! I didn't realize you were here." Tessa says rounding the corner and seeing me on the floor.

"Sorry, I was coming in to say hello but your guard dog stopped me." I joke.

"Dinner is ready kids, I was just coming to see when you'd be here." Tessa explains with a smile.

"No worries. Can I wash my hands somewhere?" I ask. I know where the bathroom is but for the sake of our secret, I pretend that I don't.

"Yup, it's right around this corner." Tessa points and tells the kids to wash their hands in the kitchen.

I head down the familiar hallway to the bathroom and clean my hands. Tessa has peppermint soap in a Santa Claus soap container and the softest bath towels I've ever felt. I make sure my neck is concealed and go back to the kitchen. Everyone is sitting and waiting for me as Tessa puts the food on the table.

"You can sit here," Tessa pulls out the chair at one end of the table. The kids are each on one side of the table and Tessa sits at the other end. "Anything you don't eat?" She asks.

"Nope, I'm happy with everything." I smile.

"How come you aren't with your family tonight?" Natalie asks.

"Natalie!" Tessa scolds.

"It's cool, my mom died a few years ago. And she was the last of my family." I explain.

"I didn't realize that." Tessa frowns.

"I don't talk about it much," I shrug. I had dealt with my grief, but part of it was talking about my mother when I could. I didn't like thinking about the end.

"You didn't have any brothers or sisters?" Drew asks.

"Nope, just me." I shrug.

"Well, I'm glad you're joining us then. No one should be alone on Christmas. Even Christmas Eve." Tessa smiles. I don't mention that I wouldn't be alone, between my friends I usually spent the holidays with them or their families.

"Are you playing Monopoly with us?" Natalie asks.

"If that's okay…" I look between her and Drew, letting it be up to them.

"Yeah, it's cool. But I'm the dog." Natalie says.

"And I'm the car." Drew says.

"I'm cool with whatever, because either way I'll win." I wink.

Everyone laughs and I feel a bit of relief. I didn't know how this would go, but I'm relieved to know it's easier than I thought. Natalie might take some time to warm up to me, but at least she was willing to get to know me. Drew was easier because he was so young and just was happy to play with someone new. I help Tessa with the dishes after dinner. The kids running off to play and call their dad.

"How come you didn't tell me about your mom?" Tessa asks catching my wrist as I hand her a plate.

"I don't know. I like talking about the living memories, to me that's how I can remember her. I don't want to think about her dying and not being here anymore." I admit.

"I understand that." She nods.

She lets go of my wrist but I lean into her, pressing my body slightly into her back. She gasps quietly, turning around only slightly to look around. I can feel my heart racing as her body melts into mine. I push her dark curls off her shoulder and lean in to whisper in her ear, "You left quite the mark on my neck Tess."

"I-I did?" She asks nervously.

"It's okay, I just wish I was able to do the same. I'd love for everyone to know you're mine." I whisper. I place a soft kiss on the nape of her neck and she shivers.

I pull away, not wanting to tempt fate and have the kids run in on us. I wanted to respect the boundary Tessa had put up. I help her bring the rest of the dishes to the sink and put them in the dishwasher. The kids come back just as we're finished holding the box of Monopoly.

"Okay, everyone pick their pieces and I'll be the banker." Tessa says as we sit down to play. She makes hot cocoa for the kids and coffee for both of us.

"Why are you the banker?" I ask.

"Drew can't do that high of math yet and Natalie can but hates to." She explains.

"Ah, well I can be the banker. I'm great with numbers." I smile.

"Sounds good to me." Tessa brings the steaming mugs over and picks the wheelbarrow as her piece.

I pick up the little hat and gather up my money. I count up everyone's starting pieces and we begin. It takes us almost three hours to finish the game. We have an apple pie for dessert that Tessa bought at the bakery in town. By the end, Drew is starting to fall asleep but refuses to leave the table. He eventually puts his head down and never picks it back up. Natalie, Tessa and I are in competitive mode but in the end, Natalie ends up winning.

"Damn! I was so close!" Tessa throws down her cards. "Okay, time for bed Drew." Tessa moves his shoulder gently and kisses his forehead.

"Oh! Actually, I brought some presents. If you guys are up for it?" I look at Natalie.

"Presents?" Drew says sleepily opening his eyes.

"You got them presents?" Tessa looks at me surprised.

"Yeah, I hope that's okay." Shit, should I have asked her first? I didn't think she'd say no to me giving them something.

"Of course, I'm just surprised. We didn't get you anything." She frowns.

"Mom, let her give us presents." Natalie adds.

"Okay, sure." Tessa laughs and we head to the living room.

Drew wakes up enough to yawn and then open his. I give Natalie and Drew theirs first, wanting to see the look on their faces as they open it. I had hoped they would like them.

"MOM! PARKER GOT ME THE NEW MINECRAFT LEGO SET! IT'S NOT EVEN OUT YET! HOW DID YOU DO THIS?!" Drew shouts excitedly. Any remnant of sleep leaving his body immediately.

"I have some connections." I wink when Tessa looks at me. Shiloh ran her own toy store, of course she could get me the most wanted toy this year two weeks early.

"Thank you so much Parker!" Drew runs over and wraps his arms around me, giving me a hug. It's quick, only giving me a second to register what's happened before he's already back to looking at the box. Tessa looks at me happily surprised, and I push down how good it feels right now.

"Wow, this is really cool." Natalie says surprised as she opens hers. I had gotten her a signed copy of the K-Pop Demon Hunters Album for a record player.

"I'll take the surprise as a compliment." I laugh.

"I just didn't think you were this cool." Natalie shrugs.

"Natalie!" Tessa scolds her and sighs.

"How did you know I had a record player?" Natalie asks. Damn, this girl was perceptive.

I couldn't admit I saw it this weekend when Tessa had showed me their rooms. "I figured every teenager these days has one." I shrugged.

"True." She smiles.

"These are really amazing gifts, I'm so sorry we didn't get you anything. It's been so crazy with the move…" Tessa frowns.

"Don't worry about it, it's the season of gift giving." I smile. "Speaking of…" I reach in the bag and hand a small package to Tessa.

"Can I…Should I open it now?" She was wondering if it was something she shouldn't open in front of the kids.

"Of course." I reassure her.

She opens the red and green tied present and inside is a silver necklace with a small book pendant. In the inside there was space to put a photo like a locket. When I saw it, I knew immediately that she would love it. She looks up at me with tears in her eyes. "It's so beautiful, oh my goodness. Thank you so much."

"I thought you could put the kids in it, so you have them with you when you're at work." I smile.

"WHAT AM I GOING IN!?" Drew turns around looking at the necklace and we all crack up as Tessa explains.

"Natalie can you help Drew brush his teeth? I want to talk to Parker for a moment." Tessa smiles.

"Sure." Natalie gets up and then looks at me. "Thank you, this is a really cool present."

"No problem, I'm glad you like it." I smile.

The kids disappear down the hallway and Tessa looks at me. "This is all too much, you didn't have to do this."

"I know, but I like giving gifts. And they loved them, so what's the harm?" I shrug.

"You really don't know how amazing you are, do you?" She asks looking at me.

"I could say the same about you." All I want to do is kiss her, but I settle for reaching for her hand and squeezing it gently. Our secret code, for wanting to do more but not being able to.

"Merry Christmas, Parker." She smiles.

"Merry Christmas Tessa," I smile.

Epilogue II

TESSA

Christmas morning is a blur like usual. Drew and Natalie ripping through presents and spending the day playing or wearing their new things. Drew got toys while Natalie got a ton of clothes and makeup. Weston finally got his shit together and took the kids for the weekend, which was filled with an awkward goodbye from his new wife. I forced a smile because it shouldn't be the kids who have to feel that. They didn't ask for their parents to break up. But the second they left I took the time to clean up the house and get ready for my date night with Parker.

We didn't have an official plan, but I knew a lot of the weekend would be spent in the new lingerie I bought. And the other half would be with the new lingerie on the floor. We figured we'd play it by ear but considering how well our first date lasted, we knew it was a possibility it would last longer than a night. So I was showered, shaved, and slipping into my holiday lingerie when Parker knocks on the door. I pull on my red long sleeved, lace robe and race to the door. The second I open the door, Parker's jaw drops.

"Holy shit." She's wearing a long winter coat I've never seen before and her legs are bare. I pull her inside before she catches a cold.

"Where are your clothes?" I ask as she pulls off her coat and then it's my turn for my jaw to drop. "Wow."

Parker's wearing this black and white slip dress that is more slip than dress. Her puckered nipples are peeking out from the thin lace fabric and I can see the outline of a thin black thong. Her red hair is curled in a near ponytail on the top of her head and she's wearing her usual pink lipstick. She's looking me over and I'm glad I decided to go all out with my lingerie. I knew she'd fuck me in anything, but there was something fun in dressing up. My lace robe had fuzzy white fur on the ends, similar to a Santa hat and under I was barely wearing anything. My red panty and bra set were virtually see through.

"I see those hickies healed up nicely." I tease looking at Parker's neck. She was stuck wearing turtle necks all week in front of the kids.

"Yes, so I would appreciate you leave your mark elsewhere. I'm running out of turtlenecks." She laughs.

I lean in to kiss her, her lips pillowing into mine. She smiles against me and I break the kiss to hold her hand. I lead her to the bedroom, feeling her eyes on my ass the whole time. I set up my room full of candles and turned off the lights to set the mood. She takes a look around and I watch her ass peeking out from the bottom of her slip. Her thighs perfectly rubbing together in a way that makes me want to be buried in them. She turns around and sits on the bed, looking up at me expectantly.

"Did you bring what we talked about?" She asks, batting her eyelashes.

"Yes," I nod and head to my dresser, retrieving the box of holiday lights.

"Are you sure you want me to…" Her voice trails.

"Oh fuck yes I do." I nod.

Dropping the box on the bed, I straddle Parker's thighs and lean in to kiss her. For a while our lips are in a frenzy with the other. It's hard seeing her all the time but not being able to touch her. I know it's for the best, I don't want the kids to know about this until it's serious. But I wish sometimes I could reach out and hold her hand or have her hug me, or vice versa. I'm sure in time things will allow it.

Parker buries her face in my chest, taking light nibbles of my breasts. She slides her hands along the white fabric of my outfit and helps me untie my robe. She does it slowly, delicately in a way that she doesn't rip it. Clearly she wants to see me in it again. I watch her bite down on her bottom lip as more of my body is exposed. I've never been self conscious about my body, I have the scars from having and carrying children but I've always been proud of my body. And the way Parker looks at me only solidifies that feeling.

"Lay on the bed, I want to tie you up." Parker commands.

It was my idea, something about being tied up with Christmas lights was always on my list. It was something Weston said was 'too adventurous' for him and made me give up. But as Parker and I divulged kinks and secret turn ons, she admitted she'd love to tie me up. So I did some research and got holiday lights that were created for this purpose. They're a bit stronger, softer wire and the lights run on a battery pack. So as I lay on the bed, my head propped up on the pillows, Parker rips open the box and unstrings them gently. She turns them on and lays them on the bed next to me.

I think she's going to tie my legs first, when she bends forward but instead she presses her lips to my panties and I moan. I was already soaked, Parker had that effect on me. And the anticipation of tonight alone was killing me. But still, she takes her time kissing, licking and teasing me through my red panties.

"Are you ready?" Parker leans up, giving me direct eye contact. I can only stare at her glistening lips and rub my thighs together at the missing friction.

"Mmm," I nod.

"Sorry babe, I need you to use your words. Are you ready?" She repeats as she picks up the lights.

"Yes." I gulp. A fire in my stomach burns hotter than ever.

"Give me your wrist." She says and I sit up, holding out my left hand for her to use. The other was basically useless, still in a cast.

Parker starts tying one of my wrists up, it's probably more complicated with one arm but she manages. Then she surprises me by climbing on the bed behind me. I can no longer see what she's doing but I can feel it all. She pulls my tied hand up over my head, and wraps the lights right around my chest. Parker leans in to kiss my cheek and then my neck softly. I relax under her touch and close my eyes.

I can feel her pulling the lights back and forth to create a knot. The warm lights touch my cool skin and the light string feels oddly like rope. She ties them around each breast, my nipples hard as can be and around my back to keep it tight. It's connected to the arm she has tied up and it's almost impossible for me to move. I don't know whether that turns me on more or it's the fact that Parker's in complete control.

"How's that feel baby?" She whispers in my ear as she tugs on the lights to pull my arm back further.

"Fuck. So good." I manage to mumble.

"Mmm, you look so pretty with these lights all over you." She murmurs and kisses my collarbone.

"I'm so fucking wet babe." I groan. I'm pushing my thighs together hoping for some kind of something.

"Maybe I should do something about that?" Parker teases, and I swear I can hear the smirk in her tone.

She pulls my arm and leaves it leaning on the headboard. She climbs out from behind me and back on the bed in front of me. I can see everything clearly and all my nerves are seconds from going off like a bomb. The lights illuminate my chest, not in an annoying way, but in a fun colorful way. The warmth from the lights is a new sensation but I like it. Parker lifts my hips, tugs off my panties and throws them to the side. The second she sees my pussy she eats like it's her last meal. I can feel myself dripping down her face but it's too good to stop. She's licking my center, sucking on my clit and holding my thighs tightly around her head. Parker looks up at me, eyes gleaming and I almost cum from that alone. This beautiful and sexy woman tongue deep in my pussy smirking at me. It should be illegal.

"Oh my God. Parker!" I want to move my arms and pull her hair, holding her still but I can't.

As I go to move my arms, the rope tugs tighter around my chest and I gasp. It's the perfect balance between pain and pleasure. Holy shit. She sucks harder on my clit and I'm whimpering for her. She could ask me anything right now and I'd do it. I was down hard for this woman and she knew it too.

"Yes! Yes! YES!" I cry out as she moves one hand to pull on the lights and then tugs on my nipple.

"Come for me baby," she breaks from sucking on my clit to say.

I can't respond with words. Only a combination of gasps and sounds as she twists my nipple and connects back to my clit. She keeps sucking on my clit as my hips buck forward and my orgasm takes me. A rush of pleasure runs through my thighs and I'm crying out her name.

"Parker! God, don't stop! Yes!" I scream. I wonder if Parker was home if she'd be able to hear me. It's not like I'm ever this loud when I'm alone though.

I expect Parker to stop as my orgasm rushes over me but she doesn't. Instead she's sliding her fingers inside me and smirking as I struggle to talk. Is she trying to make me cum again? I didn't think that was possible, but with the way her fingers move in and out of me and the rope tugs at my skin, I can already feel another orgasm building. The heat in my stomach rises and I know this one is going to be even faster than the last. Holy fucking shit. Parker brushes her thumb across my super sensitive clit and I combust.

"Oh fuck! Parker! Yes! Yes!" I scream, this time leaving me breathless. My hand tied over my head, my breasts heaving as I try to catch my breath.

"Wow, I love it when you come." She smirks before planting a brief kiss on my lips and disappearing behind me to undo the lights. She somehow manages to undo them fairly quickly and I stretch my arm out back to normal.

"Holy shit." Is all I can manage when I'm finally free. There are imprints of the lights rope and the actual lights on my skin. It looks pretty cool honestly.

"Here, have some water." She grabs the glass off my nightstand and helps me drink it. "Come lay with me a minute," She says as she puts the glass back and lays down.

I lay down next to her, my body still buzzing from the multiple orgasms. She brushes my hair out of my eyes and runs her fingernails down the sides of my arm. Parker leans in and kisses me softly. First on the cheek, then on the other, then finally on the lips. My breathing is back to normal and I watch my girlfriend in awe.

"You should give a girl a warning before you almost kill her with orgasms." I joke.

"You should always be on alert with me. And two is just getting started." She smirks.

I laugh, relaxing in her arms as she smiles at me. I know there's nothing to worry about when I'm tangled up in bed with Parker.

BONUS Epilogue

PARKER

1 year later…

"Mom! Mom! Santa came! Wake up!" Drew knocks on the door to the bedroom.

I roll over and yawn, looking at Tessa. She's still fast asleep, so I kiss her nose and then her cheeks and finally her lips before she wakes with a smile. At this point, the kids were used to me staying over and they knew I'd be here for Christmas morning this year.

"Mmm, what is it?" Tessa asks still blissfully unaware of her impatient son outside the bedroom door.

"Drew's awake, and Santa came so he's excited. We have to get up." I smile.

Tessa groans but sits up in bed and stretches. The sheet falls off her chest and I admire her breasts, I bend down to kiss each of her hardened nipples and she pushes me off her gently.

"If you start that, I'll never get out of here." She shakes her head with a laugh.

Nodding, I get out of bed and throw on the matching

pajamas Tessa got us. Apparently it was a family tradition and this year I was apart of it. They were red flannels with matching slippers and everyone had a Santa hat to wear too. I pull mine on over my red curls and wait for Tessa to finish getting dressed. By the time we open the door, Drew is bursting with energy.

"Come on!" He drags both our hands down the hallway toward the living room.

Natalie is already sitting on the couch waiting with three steaming coffee mugs. It took awhile, but she warmed up to me the way I had hoped she would. Neither of the kids were surprised by our relationship. I had been hanging out with them for months before Tessa decided to tell them. I think they were more worried they'd be moving again, but Tessa reassured them they were staying for the long haul. They'd both adjusted nicely and made a bunch of friends in school. Their dad took them twice a month on the weekends. It wasn't as much as Tessa had hoped, but at least it was something.

"I made coffee, since Drew said he couldn't wait." Natalie smiles handing us each a mug.

"Thank you," I praise her and take a seat on the couch next to her. Taking a sip, it's exactly how I liked it. We had a habit of making breakfast for each other but it was still nice Natalie took the time to know how I take my coffee.

Tessa sits down on the other while Drew sits on the floor to start opening presents. I knew what most of them were, working with Shiloh to help get the greatest and latest sets. He still believed in Santa, so we acted surprised by each unwrapped item. When he was done, he starts opening all his toys and Natalie takes a turn. Most of it is stuff she picked out herself, I mean what 14 year old wanted clothes their mom picked out for them?

"This is sort of from all of us." Natalie hands me a small bag with red tissue paper sticking out and red glitter all over the sides.

I put down my cup of coffee, and open the bag. Inside was a small-ish box with a bow on the top. I pop it open and inside is a keychain with a single silver key. On the keychain it reads '*Honorary Williams*'. My eyes immediately start to well up, did this mean what I thought it meant? Tessa and I had talked casually about moving in together. Not that it would be a huge change, but that it ultimately was up to the kids if they were okay with it. I got that, I didn't want to be some stranger moving in, I wanted them to know this was real.

"We all talked about it, and we'd love it if you moved in with us." Tessa says smiling from across the coffee table.

"Really?" I ask quietly, the tears slipping from my cheeks.

"Yes, you're already here all the time." Natalie shrugs like it's no big deal, but I can see under her icy teenager exterior.

"Here," Drew hands me a tissue and I smile.

"I'd love to." I wipe my eyes and Drew hugs me tightly. Natalie and Tessa join in too.

I excuse myself to wash my face but Tessa follows me. I'm in the bathroom, crying my eyes out when she sits on the toilet looking at me nervously.

"You don't have to say yes if you don't want to…"

"No, I'm crying happy tears I swear." I smile.

"Oh!"

"I just didn't think you moving in next door would bring me so much joy. You and the kids, you're my family and I am really glad you all feel the same about me." I sob.

Tessa stands up and pulls me in for a hug. I catch a glimpse of myself in the mirror and I look ridiculous. A grown woman in a Santa hat and matching pjs hugging another woman while tears run down their face. I start laughing and Tessa pulls away to look at me, but for some reason that only makes me laugh harder.

"Are you okay?" She asks hesitantly but I can only point at the mirror.

"I swear I'm just tired. And incredibly happy." I smile. "But just so you know, I don't plan on being an honorary Williams for long." I wink.

Tessa raises an eyebrow and then smiles, "Oh yeah?"

"Trust me baby, I know what I'm getting myself tangled up in. And I wouldn't have it any other way." I say before leaning in to kiss her.

Acknowledgments

To my little bear, Teddy for giving me vast knowledge about Minecraft. Since I otherwise wouldn't have anywhere to put all these fun facts, I created 'Drew' as a memory of you. My memory is terrible and I know twenty years from now I'll be missing the days when all you talked about was Minecraft and laughed when I got things wrong. Thank you for being authentically you. I love you.

To my readers, I thank all of you every single day. I couldn't do this without your constant and consistent support. It's been almost five years of me doing what I love professionally, and it still feels like a dream. From all of you who supported me since the first Christmas romance, to those starting out with me here, I'm forever grateful.

Also by Shannon O'Connor

SEASONS OF SEASIDE SERIES

(each book can be read as a standalone)

Only for the Summer

Only for Convenience

Only for the Holidays

Only to Save You

Seasons of Seaside: The Complete Collection

LIGHTHOUSE LOVERS

(each book can be read as a standalone)

Tour of Love

Hate to Love You

To Be Loved

Inn Love

Love, Unexpected

ETERNAL PORT VALLEY SERIES

Unexpected Departure

Unexpected Beginnings & Endings

Unexpected Days

Eternal Port Valley: The Complete Collection

STANDALONES

Electric Love

Butterflies in Paris

All's Fair in Love & Vegas

Fumbling into You

Doll Face

Poolside Love

BEHIND THE SCENES

(each book can be read as a standalone)

Eras of Us

Not My Fault

Bad at Love

EVERGREEN VALLEY

(each book can be read as a standalone)

Tangled Up In You

How the B*tch Stole Christmas

Santa, Baby

SAPPHIRE FALLS ORCHARD

(each book can be read as a standalone)

Sweater Weather

Accidentally Falling

THE HOLIDAYS WITH YOU

(each book can be read as a standalone)

I Saw Mommy Kissing the Nanny

Lucky to be Yours

The Only Reason

Ugly Sweater Christmas

POETRY

For Always

Holding on to Nothing

Say it Everyday

Midnights in a Mustang

About the Author

Shannon O'Connor is a twenty something, bisexual, self published author of several poetry books and counting. She released her debut contemporary romance novel, *Electric Love* in 2021. O'Connor is continuously working on new poetry projects, book reviews, and more, while also diving into motherhood. When she's not reading or writing she can be found watching Disney movies with her son where they reside in New York. She is currently a full time mom and full time author.

She sometimes writes as S O'Connor for MF romances and as Shannon Renee for Poly romances.

Heat. Heart. & HEA's.

Check out more work & updates on:
Facebook Group: https://www.facebook.com/groups/shanssquad

Website: https://shanoconnor.com

facebook.com/AuthorShanOConnor

instagram.com/authorshannonoconnor

bookbub.com/authors/shannon-o-connor

pinterest.com/Shannonoconnor1498

threads.com/@authorshannonoconnor